"THE BLACK FOG"

AIRSHIP 27 PRODUCTIONS

The Purple Scar Volume Three

"The Black Fog" ©2018 Gene Moyers

Published by Airship 27 Productions
www.airship27.com
www.airship27hangar.com

Interior illustrations ©2018 Chris Kohler
Cover illustration ©2018 Graham Hill

Editor: Ron Fortier
Associate Editor: Jonathan Sweet
Marketing and Promotions Manager: Michael Vance
Production and design by Rob Davis.

ISBN-13: 978-1-946183-38-5
ISBN-10: 1-946183-38-5

Printed in the United States of America

10 9 8 7 6 5 4 3 2 1

THE PURPLE SCAR

VOLUME THREE

"THE BLACK FOG"

BY GENE MOYERS

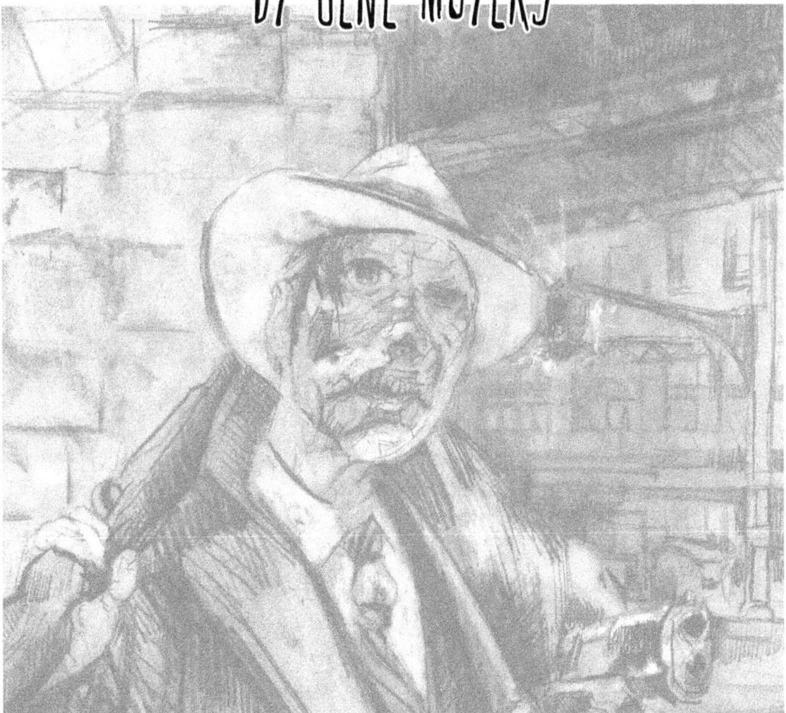

CHAPTER ONE

"Oh...it's just what I was looking for!"

The middle aged sales woman smiled indulgently, "It's very nice madam. I'm sure your husband will think it's stunning."

Dale Jordan looked at herself in the mirror the women's boutique owner had thoughtfully placed on the counter. She reached up to her head and adjusted the tilt of the new red hat perched on her long, lush, reddish-brown hair. The mirror reflected her emerald green eyes and perfect complexion. Deciding the hat was perfect, she turned to the sales woman and smiled, "I'll take it." She held up her left hand and wiggled her fingers, "And I'm not married yet, just engaged."

The woman nodded knowingly, "I'm sure you'll be married soon enough when your fiancé sees you in that new blue dress you bought. I'll wrap your hat if you'd like."

Dale waved a hand negligently, "I think I'll wear it. Although I do believe it needs a pin or two to keep it from blowing off." While the woman wrapped up the rest of her purchases, Dale made sure her hat was firmly pinned in place. When her bill was ready she paid the woman, accepted her change and slung her purse over her left arm. She then took up her packages and turned toward the door, "Thank you for your help. You've been most kind."

The woman bustled forward, "Here, let me get that door for you." She held the door as Dale passed through and added, "Thank you so much and please come again."

As Dale stepped from the cool of the store into the humid air under the shadow of the store's awning she was nearly knocked to the ground by a man running past. She leaned back barely keeping her balance as the hatless man, his jacket flapping open dashed past. Her angry admonishment was cut off by the sudden, loud crash of shattering glass. She jerked her head around; across the street she was shocked to see a roughly dressed man reach through the shattered plate glass window of an appliance store and pick up a radio.

The sales clerk behind her gave a cry and slammed the door shut. Dale heard the lock click. She looked left hoping to sight a patrolman walking his beat but the screech of tires on asphalt and a scream pulled her attention back toward the right. Shocked she nearly dropped her packages at the sight of the busy downtown street. Perhaps a hundred feet away a wall of Blackness covered the width of the street from building to building. The Blackness was like a wall that ran vertically from the ground upwards to perhaps thirty feet or more. At first Dale thought it was a solid wall of some kind that had mysteriously appeared. Then she saw it bulge and boil forward slightly. It was then she realized the black curtain was gaseous like an impossible black fog.

As she watched a sedan careened blindly out of the Blackness. It jumped the sidewalk nearly hitting a woman fleeing the black fog and struck a mailbox. The red and blue box was torn from its anchors and flew across the sidewalk nearly striking a poorly dressed man carrying an armful of shoe boxes. He dove for safety, the boxes flying out of his arms scattering the new shoes across the sidewalk. Dale was stunned. More people were spilling out of the Blackness running in terror.

Dale was rudely jerked from her stunned fixation by the crashing of glass. Thirty feet to her left two men were climbing through a smashed store window. Dale began backing away in horror. A scream came from across the street. There a well-dressed woman was tugging desperately on the strap of her purse. A roughly dressed man on the other end gave a sharp jerk and the woman was pulled off her feet. The man turned and ran away hugging the purse to his chest. Dale started across the street toward the fallen woman. As she did she was forced to dodge terrified people running out of the Blackness.

Before Dale could reach her, the downed woman got to her feet, glanced over her shoulder in fear and ran up the street. Dale stopped in the middle of the street and was immediately brushed hard by a running man. Spun around, Dale was shocked to see that the Blackness had advanced nearly forty feet closer. Her heart beating loudly in her chest she immediately began backing away. After a few steps she turned and began to run. As she did she was aware of the chaos around her. Oncoming cars were stopped in the street as their drivers abandoned them and fled. People spilled out of store fronts and ran westward fearfully glancing over their shoulders as they did. Others, mostly men were occupied by looting businesses. There was glass everywhere and the street and sidewalks were cluttered with dropped packages, hats, even discarded shoes. Dale worked her way back onto the sidewalk as she reached the first of the stalled cars. She was jostled and shoved by other fleeing refugees. As she passed the shattered window of a dress store a woman jumped out carrying an armload of dresses. Dale was caught broadside and knocked to the ground.

She landed hard on her right hip. The looter then stumbled over her and fell hard, the dresses spilling over both of them. Biting her lip to keep from cursing Dale fought from under the pile of clothes in time to see the woman scramble to her feet, grab a handful of dresses and flee. On her knees Dale gathered her packages. As she got to her feet she realized the Blackness was no more than thirty feet away. Suddenly terrified, she dropped her packages and turned to run.

It was nearly six o'clock and the sun was close to the horizon. Dale raised her hand to shield her eyes from the glare of the setting sun as she ran west along the street. The streets seemed filled with frantic people all running along and ahead of her. Glancing behind she could see the advancing wall of Blackness. She could hear multiple sirens getting louder by the second. Fighting her way to a corner she leaned against the pole of a traffic signal. People were still running everywhere in terror. The sound of breaking glass and metal clanging from minor accidents filled the air.

Dale had lost her packages but managed to hang onto her purse. As she watched, across the intersection, a police cruiser bumped its way up onto the sidewalk to get around stalled cars. It reached the intersection and two officers jumped out. One drew his night stick and ran to a shattered store front and climbed in to struggle with a looter. The other ran to help a woman who had fallen in the street. Dale started toward them but as she did movement to her right caught her eye. A roughly dressed man with a black hood over his head had appeared out of the edge of the black fog. He appeared to carry something on his back. Apparently surprised he immediately turned and disappeared back into the wall of Blackness.

Startled, Dale hesitated for a moment then turned to reach the police officer and tell him of the hooded man she had just seen. He was busy blowing his whistle and waving his arms. Two more officers were running toward him. Changing her mind, Dale instead took a limping woman by the arm and led her away. The two reached the far curb as the darkness rolled over the intersection. Dale yelled at the woman, "Run!"

She followed her advice and ran as fast as she could away from the approaching Blackness. Just then the heel of her left shoe broke. She turned her ankle, tripped and went down to her knees, scraping one badly. As she attempted to get to her feet a man running past crashed into her. Both of them went down. Dale was stunned for a moment as the man scrambled off her with a curse. As she attempted to once more get to her feet she realized how the light was fading. Startled she looked up as the wall of Blackness swept over her. Dale opened her mouth to cry for help but it was drowned out by other screams.

Doctor Miles Murdock set his glass down and picked up the newspaper. As usual the news was all bad. The war news was the worst. Things were bad in Europe and not much better in the Far East. But the big news was that Congress had just voted in the draft. With all the new jobs created the last few years by the new defense contracts, unemployment had already been going down. Now with a draft Miles figured that would just about put an end to the unemployed. He turned a page. Ah…the weather forecast hadn't changed. More hot and humid weather was predicted. Miles smiled wryly as he ran his hand through his wavy, black hair. It was a bit late in the year for this kind of weather; the air was so humid you could almost cut it with a knife.

He shook his head and turned to election news. With the election barely a month away things were heating up. Mayor Morningham was in a tight race with not one but two challengers on the city council. Councilman Ross was a long shot but Councilman Paley was making a lot of noise challenging Morningham. A recent arrival in Akelton, he was young and aggressive and people seemed in the mood for change. Miles was a firm backer of the Mayor and had even donated a decent amount to his re-election campaign. That contribution had netted Miles with an invitation to the opening of the new historical museum tomorrow. Miles was looking forward to the outing although he figured Dale and he would have to sit through more than one boring speech.

Speaking of Dale…Miles looked at his wrist watch and wondered where she was. He had closed up the Down Street clinic promptly at five so that he could meet her here for dinner. Pleading that she just had to buy a new hat for tomorrow's event she had taken part of the afternoon off to go shopping. It was nearly six o'clock and Doc Miles had expected her by now. As he pondered he could hear a siren in the street outside. The volume increased rapidly and then decreased just as rapidly as the vehicle passed the restaurant.

Miles got up to use the restroom. When he returned to his table another siren was rapidly approaching. As it passed, its siren was replaced by yet another getting louder by the second. Doc frowned as he took his seat. Looking around he noticed other patrons had taken notice of the commotion. Many were craning their heads around toward the street. A few had actually got up and were drifting toward the front of the restaurant. As more sirens sounded loudly out on the street Doc got up and pushed his way through the rapidly growing crowd to the front door. He squeezed past a couple of rubberneckers and managed to reach the sidewalk. People gathered nervously on the sidewalk looking frightened. It was near sunset. The sun had dropped behind tall buildings to the west leaving the streets in shadow. As Doc watched, yet another emergency vehicle screamed past. The ambulance flew past him siren blaring, made a left at the corner and head further downtown. Miles looked that way and saw what appeared to be a cloud of black smoke rising over nearby buildings and slowly dispersing as it rose.

Grimly, Doc sprinted in the direction the ambulance had gone. A fire in one of the tall buildings downtown would be a catastrophe ...and Dale was somewhere that way.

On hands and knees Dale was completely disoriented in the total Blackness. She could hear the sounds of panic everywhere around her. There were curses, screams and somewhere nearby a woman was crying. She could also hear sirens and whistles and angry shouts. Surprisingly she could breathe normally. Somehow she had expected the Blackness to be some kind of choking smoke or gas but she found she could breathe as if she was standing in clear air. She tried to get to her feet and was immediately knocked back down as someone tripped over her. She heard someone grunt as they landed heavily and heard a man's curses receding away. Staying on her knees Dale moved slowly until her head bumped against something solid. Reaching out a hand she felt smooth metal. It was the fender of an auto. Using it as support she pulled herself to her feet.

To her left a whistle sounded loudly. Dale moved slowly that way holding an arm out in front of her like a blind man. She nearly tripped when she stepped suddenly down a curb but recovered. Her purse slipped off her shoulder to hang from its strap off her forearm. She was surprised to realize she had somehow hung onto it. Hearing a man's voice giving commands somewhere close by and she moved toward the sound. Soon she realized that it was a police officer. He seemed to be gathering people around him in the darkness. He was urging calm and periodically blowing his whistle to attract attention. Dale nearly sobbed with relief when she bumped into the back of a woman. There were people gathered all around the officer. A crying woman grasped her arm. Dale spoke reassuringly to her unseen companion. They were safe for at least the moment.

Traffic was heavy but slow. Doc dodged honking cars and continued running in the direction the sirens were going. He soon reached a point where stalled cars filled the street. Drivers stood next to their vehicles staring at the towering wall of Blackness two blocks ahead. Others pushed past Doc in the opposite direction joining an exodus of hundreds running away in terror as he stood petrified for a moment staring at the wall of Blackness filling the street ahead. Police officers had abandoned their cruisers and were pushing their way forward blowing whistles and shouting for calm. Doc followed a pair of officers who were shoving and using their night sticks as needed.

Finally Doc broke out into a relatively clear intersection. The Blackness formed a wall from one side of the street to the other a block ahead. The intersection had become a casualty collection point. Injured people were lying on the ground. Firemen and ambulance attendants moved among them giving first aid. Doc wildly scanned the crowd. He knew it would be sheer chance to see Dale among the hundreds of milling, fleeing and dazed people. He desperately wanted to continue into the crowds searching for his beloved but he knew he would never find her…and the cries of the injured tore at his ears. Deciding, he gritted his teeth and pushed toward a row of injured lying on the ground in front of him.

+++

Linking hands the blinded refugees moved forward, threading their way through stalled cars invisible in the darkness. Dale wasn't sure how far they traveled before she tripped over something and fell again scraping her knee. She attempted to rejoin the retreating voices but couldn't locate them in the Blackness. She finally continued creeping down the street moving from stalled vehicle to vehicle. She rationalized that she was at least moving…hopefully in the right direction. There was a one in four chance that she was moving back into the heart of the Blackness instead of away but there was nothing else to do.

Minutes passed. Voices and yells diminished. Dale wasn't sure if this was good or bad. She continued moving forward because there was nothing else to do. Moments later the Blackness seemed to lighten and then with the suddenness of a door opening in a blacked out room she stumbled out into the twilight of an Akelton street.

Disoriented for a moment Dale looked around. She was near an intersection crowded with abandoned cars. Stunned people moved aimlessly about. In the intersection, several police officers were blowing whistles and waving people toward them. Gratefully Dale stumbled that way. When she reached them they ignored her but kept chanting and pointing, "This way folks. Move slowly. Help is this way."

She turned and worked her way down a side street, just one of many refugees. Near the end of the next block, firemen and white coated men and women were helping people. As Dale stumbled that way a fireman grabbed her by the arm and steered her toward an ambulance. Dale protested that she was fine but the fire fighter said gently, "Don't worry ma'am. We'll get that head looked at right away." Dale lifted a hand to her face and only then realized she was bleeding from a wound on her forehead. Dried blood coated her cheek. She relaxed and allowed herself to be led to the back of an open ambulance. She had to wait a few minutes but finally she was seated on the rear bumper and a nurse began to attend to her.

His jacket off Doc worked over an unconscious man. The man was bleeding from a head wound. Doc had managed to stop the bleeding and roughly bandaged it using the sleeve torn from his dress shirt. Unfortunately he could tell the man was going into shock. He quickly loosened the man's tie and shirt collar. He then removed the victim's shoes. He placed them under the man's feet to elevate them slightly. He then grabbed his own discarded suit jacket and covered the man as best he could with it. Many injured could survive their injuries but would die of shock if not quickly treated.

Doc felt a hand on his shoulder and looked up into the face of a man carrying a black medical bag. Doc knew him. The man was a staff member at City Hospital near his Down Street clinic in one Akleton's poorer districts. The doctor asked, "What's the situation Miles?"

Doc blew out a breath and replied, "Concussion. I don't think his skull is fractured but he has been unconscious since I arrived. He's going into shock; he needs fluids and evacuation a soon as possible."

His colleague nodded as he knelt and opened his black bag, "Good work, doctor. I'll take over now."

Doc nodded gratefully and stood up. Looking around he could see that Akelton's well trained emergency services were getting a handle on things. More police, firemen and medical personnel were arriving by the moment. Across the intersection Doc could swear that the wall of Blackness was beginning to thin. He moved toward two ambulances parked side by side with people gathered around them looking of more victims to help.

It was then he saw her. Dale was just standing up and thanking a nurse. She was dirty. Her skirt was torn as was one sleeve of her formerly white blouse. Her stocking were in shreds. Both knees were skinned and she was wearing a small bandage over her right eye. She was also wearing a new hat that though tilted over at an alarming angle still clung tenaciously to her head. Doc thought she was the most beautiful sight he had ever seen.

He brushed through the crowd and stopped six feet away and smiled widely, "I like your hat." Dale looked up and her mouth fell open. Her face crumpling into tears she threw herself forward into Doc's open arms.

Doc sat on a bus stop bench holding Dale's hand. Fifteen minutes had passed since they had found one another. The Blackness had rapidly begun to disperse as quickly as it appeared. Visibility was no better though. With the sun now fully down, darkness was rapidly falling over downtown Akelton. Street lights had begun to activate. Minutes before Detective Captain Dan Griffin had arrived at the head of a phalanx of his plain clothes detectives. Barking orders he quickly dispatched his men to help the emergency personnel. Doc sat with his arm around his rumpled fiancé. Once he had made sure she was unharmed except for minor injuries the two had quickly traded stories.

Doc was very interested in her account. From the talk he was hearing around him it appeared that Dale had been near the center of whatever the Blackness was. He was especially interested in her account of the aggressive looters. He also questioned her closely on another topic, "So this hooded man was carrying something. Could it have been stolen loot?"

"It didn't look that way, Miles. It looked more like some kind of bulky backpack from the way he was carrying it. I'm sorry I couldn't get a better look at it but things were a little confused."

"I can imagine. And he was the only hooded person you saw."

"Only the one. Uh oh, here comes Captain Dan, and he doesn't look happy."

Nor should he be, Doc thought as he stood up and held out his hand to police Captain Daniel Griffin. Griffin took the hand and shook it heartily, "It's good to see you safe Miles." The square jawed, square shouldered detective turned to Dale and bent over gently touching her shoulder, "I'm terribly sorry that you were mixed up in this tragedy, Dale." His face darkened as he looked over her appearance, "I'm going to get to the bottom of this as soon as possible."

He turned back as Doc spoke, "What the devil was that black stuff, Dan?"

Griffin shrugged, "All I have are reports. You were as close as anybody. What do you think, Miles?"

Doc waved a hand, "I got here just in time to start clearing up the mess. I only saw the Blackness from a distance, but Dale was right in it from the beginning." Both men turned to the pretty nurse. Dale quickly repeated her experiences to Griffin. His mouth tightened and his fists clenched as he listened to her tale of fear and chaos. When Dale had finished he asked, "Was it some kind of smoke screen?"

"No, definitely not. When I was totally enveloped in it, I could breathe just fine. It was as if…as if the very air had turned black."

Doc looked thoughtful, "Like fog on a very dark night."

"Something like that but visibility was totally gone. I couldn't see my hand in front of my face."

Doc took Dale's hand and pulled her to her feet, "Dan, Dale needs to get some rest. I'm going home. I won't be at home later but I'll talk to you in the morning."

Griffin gave Doc a sharp look and a quick nod, "Be careful out there. I'll be up all night trying to sort things out. Hopefully I'll have more in the morning."

The three quickly said their good byes and Doc led Dale back toward the restaurant and his roadster. Griffin was serious in his warning to Doc. Griffin was one of only three people in the world who knew that Doctor Miles Murdock was more than a highly talented plastic surgeon. He had an alter ego, one who would be prowling Akelton's streets that night searching for answers to the mysterious Blackness in guise of the mysterious Purple Scar.

When they reached his car Doc drove them to his apartment located above his Swank Street clinic. This clinic was where Doc ministered to wealthy clients. He was well known as one of the finest plastic surgeons in the country. Wealthy patients came from far and wide to avail themselves of his services. Their payments paid for his apartment and supported him, but more importantly their payments funded his clinic on Down Street in the heart of one of the city's poorest districts. There he saw patients regardless of their circumstances or assets. He had helped hundreds of unfortunate people lead better lives.

Doc's upstairs apartment was well appointed and comfortable. In addition to his living quarters there was a well-equipped gym that Doc used every day to keep himself in top shape, as well as a full art studio. Doc was a talented sculptor. He used this skill to model his patient's injuries and assist them in their healing.

Waiting in the living room when Doc and Dale arrived was the third person privy to Doc's secret. Tommy Pedlar was a rather small, thin, middle aged man with thinning hair. Tommy's looks were deceiving. He had been a talented second story man in his day. Now his sole job was serving as Doc's friend, aide and "legs." Tommy knew every stoolie and low life in town. He was Doc's eyes and ears on the street.

Now the little man came forward looking concerned, "Doc, where you been. I've been worried sick. I heard about the riot downtown and . . ." His voice trailed off as he took in Dale's worse for wear appearance and Doc's coatless suit.

Doc led Dale to a sofa and turned, "I know all about the riot Tommy. I'm afraid we got caught up in it. What's the news on the radio?"

"Just news about the riot; descriptions of damage and what not. Also some talk about a black fog rolling over downtown."

Doc quickly filled Tommy in on their adventures then finished with, "Now we have work to do."

Tommy nodded, "Whatever you want Doc." Tommy's loyalty to Doc was unquestioned. Years before his young daughter Janie had been horribly scarred in an automobile accident. Doc had used all his skill and now little Janie lived a normal and healthy life. When Doc's older brother, a police officer, had been brutally murdered Tommy had been indispensable in helping Doc find his killer. Realizing that there was more work to be done bringing criminals like those who had slain his brother to justice, Doctor Murdock had taken on the disguise of his murdered brother's death mask and set out to become Akelton's protector. He had paid to send Tommy's little daughter away to boarding school and enlisted Tommy and his nurse Dale in his crusade.

He had fought and defeated many criminals. The entire Akelton underworld was now wary of the terrifying masked avenger. They knew that the streets were prowled after dark by the Purple Scar. Ordinary crime he left to police but high profile or violent crimes were sure to draw the attention of the fearsome avenger. The underworld knew what had happened to many of their colleagues who had crossed his path.

Doc strode through his apartment to his private study with Tommy close behind. Going to a hidden safe Doc quickly dialed the combination. When it was open he began pulling out various items. Meanwhile he called out instructions, "Tommy, I want you to go out and hit as many bars, diners, pool halls and any other places as you can think of. Find out what people on the street know or think about tonight's chaos. I want facts, theories, rumors; anything you hear." He glanced at his wrist watch, "I'll be back here by midnight. We'll compare notes then."

Tommy nodded, "Gotcha boss, if there's anything to hear, I'll get it." He immediately turned and headed for the back stairs leading down to the concealed entrance that led to an alley on another street.

When his aide was gone Doc went to his bedroom and changed into a cheaper, dark suit. He then stopped to talk to Dale, "I don't want you going home tonight. Use my bed. Get some rest. I'll be gone for a while but you'll be safe here."

Dale looked at him knowingly, "And the Purple Scar...?"

"He'll be getting to the bottom of this mess if he can." He touched Dale's nose with the tip of one finger. Dale smiled and Doc turned on his heel. Stopping in is study he picked up the items from his safe. His .38 revolver went into a holster on his hip. A handful of cartridges went into his pants pocket along with his ring of master keys. A pocket flashlight went into his jacket pocket along with his black leather gloves. Lastly he picked up two pliable, close fitting masks. One was a dark purplish color and had terribly scarred features. This went into a concealed pocket inside his jacket. The other mask was of man with average forgettable features and mousy brown hair. This mask Doc pulled on over his own face. Carefully adjusting it he looked like every tired working man in town.

The disguised Doc left via the back stairway. Through the alley he exited onto another nearby street where he walked to a bus stop. Ten minutes wait rewarded him with a seat on a bus crowded with working people returning home for the night. The Scar leaned back and closed his eyes pretending to doze. Actually he was listening to his fellow passengers. They seemed somewhat subdued. He heard a few low voiced comments about the events downtown but there was certainly little gossip or anyone speculating about the day's events.

He got off the bus in a working class neighborhood and made his way to a coffee shop. There he ordered coffee and settled in. His coffee arrived and realizing he had missed dinner he ordered a sandwich to go with it. In the half hour he loitered there he heard similar hushed comments about the Blackness and near riot downtown. Apparently word had spread quickly but people seemed surprised and unsure of what it all meant. Few of the frightened people voiced theories on what was behind it all.

The Scar left the diner and walked the neighborhood. He found a fairly busy bar. Inside he ordered a beer and kept his ears open but again heard no interesting rumors or talk. Whatever was behind tonight's chaos was a total surprise to most of Akelton. As he got up to leave, the disguised physician hoped Tommy was having better luck.

The Scar then hopped a late night bus and took it to a shadier part of town. Once there he walked the streets until he found the business he was looking for. He chanced a quick look inside the *High Point Bar*. It was crowded as usual and it took a minute for him to spot the man he was looking for. Assured of his quarry's presence he ducked out into the shadowy street. Spotting a dark opening across the street, he crossed over and stepped into the deep shadows of an alley. The street was empty and he was unseen.

He removed his hat and quickly slipped his mask off. He secreted it in a hidden pocket in his coat and pulled out the purple colored mask. He pulled this mask over his head to replace the anonymous face with the horrid features of the fearsome Purple Scar. Replacing his hat the Scar quickly pulled out his revolver and checked its load. Re-holstering it he pulled on his gloves, took up a spot near the mouth of the alley and waited.

Time passed. Men entered the *High Point* and some left. But not the man the Purple Scar was waiting for. Then nearly an hour later, a man exited the bar. The Scar stiffened, "Slick" Willie Morton; small time bookie and general low life was the man he was after tonight. Willie loitered outside the door of the bar lighting a cigarette. The Scar glanced both ways and stepped out of the alley. He crossed street silently on his soft soled shoes and stepped into a darkened doorway. Moments later a man in working clothes and a leather jacket stepped out of the *High Point* looked around and moved up to Willie. As the Scar watched he passed something quickly to the bookie. The Scar drew his revolver, stepped out onto the sidewalk and grated out harshly, "Willie Morton." The two men spun around in shocked alarm.

The Purple Scar raised his arm and pointed his revolver at the two. The stranger gaped at the horribly scarred avenger and dropped a piece of paper on the sidewalk. His hands shot into the air. Willie dropped something as well and held up his empty hands in front of him and gasped, "Don't shoot Scar! I'm clean." There was a moment of frozen silence before the Scar stepped forward and toed the bills on the ground in front of him, "So you're not making book for your friend?" He pointed his revolver at the second man and rasped out, "You like to bet? You just made a bad one. You lose. Now go, before I decide I don't like you." He reached forward and grabbed Willie by the lapel with his free hand and whispered harshly, "We need to talk, Willie."

The second man backed away a terrified look on his face. When he was twenty feet away he turned and took to his heels. The Scar pulled Willie down the block and shoved him into a doorway. He put his gloved hand on his chest and pushed him up against the door. Willie managed to stutter, "Wha...what do you want?"

The Purple Scar leaned in until his scarred visage was inches from Willie's face and whispered harshly, "I need answers Willie. I want to know who's behind the riot downtown tonight."

Willie gulped, "Uh, how should I know?"

The Scar brought his revolver up and gently touched the barrel to the end of Willie's nose, "I know you make book for O'Brian. You know what's going on out there."

"No, Scar. Honest. You shot up O'Brian's boys so bad last spring they're still laying low. I'm just . . ."

Scar thumbed back the hammer of his gun and grated; "Don't lie to me! I want to know what you've heard."

"You like to bet? You just made a bad one."

Even in the dim light Scar could see Willie go pale, "I ain't heard nothin. Everybody's talking about the riot and that weird black fog but nobody knows nothin."

"Nobody bragging? No whispers? Nothing?"

"No Scar. I swear it."

The Purple Scar could see the little man was sweating and he believed him. He decided to let him go…for now, "Alright Willie. You can go. But I'll be back…soon. When I do you better know something, got it?"

Willie gulped and looked relieved, "Yes sir. I got it."

"Good. Walk away." He grabbed Willie by the shoulder and pushed him east on the sidewalk. Willie walked slowly away. After a few tentative steps he looked over his shoulder but the man in the scarred mask was gone.

Less than an hour later the Scar stood in the shadows outside a shop. As he watched, the three lighted balls illuminating the entrance and marking it as a pawn shop went out. He looked at his watch; just after eleven o'clock. Minutes later the door opened and a man in an overcoat exited. As he turned and locked the door the Scar stepped up to him. "Closing early, Jimmy?"

Startled by the grating voice behind him Jimmy "Cash" McCall jerked so hard he dropped his keys to the sidewalk. He spun around and stepped back in fear, his back against the closed door of his shop, "The Purple Scar! What do you want? I told you I'm not fencing stuff anymore. I'm out of that game."

Scar walked closer and pointed a gloved finger at the pawn shop owner, "You're not fencing jewelry anymore but I know you're still taking in cheap stuff on the side. You're also giving out high interest loans to half the stoolies and lowlifes in town."

Cash McCall grimaced and tried to look insulted, "Hey, there's no harm in making a few friendly loans."

"I don't care about loan sharking to other lowlifes. But right now I'm interested in what you hear from your customers. I need information."

McCall looked visibly relieved, "Well, in that case, sure…I'm glad to help out."

The Scar poked him in the chest hard with his gloved finger, "Don't fool with me McCall or you'll find yourself running your business face down in the river! Now talk! Tell me what you know about the riot downtown tonight. There must be somebody talking about it."

McCall looked surprised for a moment, then he shook his head, "I heard about it on the radio…and a couple of customers mentioned it but that's all. I don't know nothin' about it."

The Scar thought this over for a moment, "So, none of the mobs are talking about a big score?"

"No Scar. I swear I haven't heard any of the usual guys talking at all."

There was a pause before the Scar whispered harshly, "Any new faces in town lately? Maybe a new gang moving in?"

McCall shook his head, "Not that I heard. None of the gangs are talking. Everything's been quiet."

The Purple Scar decided that McCall was telling the truth. He stepped back and slipped his gun back beneath his jacket, "Okay McCall, I believe you. But I'll be back if I don't find anything elsewhere." He took a step back, turned and disappeared quickly down the darkened sidewalk.

McCall bent forward to retrieve his keys then straightened up and wiped his hand across his face. He let out a long breath and muttered, "I need a drink." Shaking his head he turned and walked quickly the other way down the darkened street resisting a strong urge to run.

From a darkened doorway near the end of the block the Scar watched McCall walk shakily away. He let McCall remain in business because his pawnshop was an important hangout for the lower criminal element. A lot of business went on in his place and a lot of gossip as well. The man behind the mask frowned; if McCall had heard nothing then no one was talking. If whoever was responsible for the Blackness and riot tonight was from out of town it would be much harder to track them.

Doc sat back in the chair at his desk. He frowned into the glass he was drinking from and took a sip. A noise out in the hall caught his ear. Moments later Tommy entered Doc's study. He flopped tiredly into an armchair as Doc spoke, "I hope you had more luck than I did tonight."

"Fraid not, Doc. A lot of people are talking out there; everybody's heard about the riot and the black fog but nobody knows nothing."

"You see any gang members out there?"

"Yeah, a few but everyone I saw that's mobbed up seemed as surprised as everybody else."

"That's about what I got, Tommy. A lot of people had heard about tonight but nobody seemed to know anything definite. I asked around about any new gangs operating in town too but came up empty there too."

Tommy nodded, "If there's a new gang behind this then they're sure laying low." He scratched his head and added, "There is one funny thing

I heard though." Doc raised an inquiring eyebrow and waited. Tommy continued, "A guy I heard talking at *Harry's* said he heard that people looking for a job should go downtown tonight; that there were going to be a lot of new jobs there."

"Really? Who was supposed to be hiring?"

"No one seemed to know. This guy just heard some of his buddies were going downtown to look for jobs on Friday afternoon." Doc thought that one over for a moment but couldn't make anything definite of it. He finally shook his head, "Well, I guess we've done everything we can for tonight. Go get some sleep. We'll see how things look in the morning.

Tommy nodded and stood up. He wished Doc goodnight and picking up his jacket left the study. Doc was about to turn off his desk light when the telephone rang. Frowning he looked at his watch. It was after midnight. Who would be calling now? He picked up the receiver and put it to his ear, "Hello."

"Hello, Doc? It's Griffin. There's been more trouble."

Suddenly alert Doc asked, "What now?"

"George Darlan has been kidnapped. A gang of men wearing black hoods showed up at his house, broke in, clubbed down a couple of servants and disappeared. Their getaway was covered by a screen of Blackness that covered the whole block where Darlan lived. By the time our boys got there it was dispersing and there was no sign of Darlan or the kidnappers."

Doc was surprised. He knew Darlan as a wealthy business man but was not personally acquainted with him. He asked Griffin, "When was this?"

"Almost two hours ago. I've been too busy cleaning up the details to call you. Have you got anything?"

"I'm afraid not, Dan. Nobody on the street is talking. Either no one knows anything or people are too afraid to talk."

"I'm worried, Miles. Darlan's kidnapping must have been planned well in advance. It's looking like this afternoon was just the first act of God knows what."

"But why Darlan?"

"I don't know. But I'm afraid this is going to get a lot worse before it gets better." Doc could only agree. The two friends said their goodbyes and hung up. He walked through his quarters turning off lights before retiring to the sofa in his living room. There, he lay awake a long time trying to make sense of the day's strange events before sleep finally overcame him.

+++

The one man who could explain everything to Miles Murdock stood in a darkened room staring into a fire burning in a large ornate brick fireplace. The tall ceilinged room behind him was in darkness. Richly paneled walls hung with paintings and a wall of books behind him hovered at the edge of the fire light hinting at wealth. He sipped from a glass of brandy and nodded to himself. Everything had gone perfectly today. The Blackness had worked perfectly. He had run large scale tests before, of course, but today it had been real. His men had performed their duties as ordered and everything had gone like clockwork. And the results had been impressive.

He had been nearby watching, of course. Murphy had urged caution but he had been unable to resist watching the chaos in person. It had been most gratifying to see people running in fear; fear of him. The thought of that fear, the chaos, the people running in terror, brought a smile to his lips.

He took another sip and thought, "Yes, it has gone well so far. Now for the next step." His thoughts turned to his prisoner. He would soon confront Darlan. Would that greedy barbarian remember? Would he suspect why he had been singled out? The man would see that he did. And then? He sipped and stared at the crackling flames lost in his memories.

CHAPTER TWO

"Well, it looks as bad in print as I thought," Doc Murdock shook his head and set down his coffee cup. Dale bit down on a piece of toast and remarked wryly, "In print? They should have been there in person!"

After a restless night on the sofa, Doc had driven Dale back to her apartment first thing in the morning. She had talked him into staying for breakfast. While he ate Doc perused the morning newspaper. The paper was playing the riot up big. The large bold print headline read 'Chaos in Downtown.' The story took up the entire front page with the exception of a story recounting the kidnapping of George Darlan. The police must be withholding news of the hooded kidnappers because the article only speculated that the kidnapping and riot were related.

Doc sighed as he dropped the paper down next to his plate. He wiped his mouth on his napkin and stood up. "I knew the papers would play up the riot big, but they make it sound as if the downtown area was burned to the ground. I guess yellow journalism is alive and well here in

Akelton." He picked up his jacket and put it on. As he did Dale came over and straightened his lapels. "You're not forgetting that we're invited to the opening of the new Historic Society Museum this afternoon, are you?"

Doc smiled, "Not at all. I just want to swing by downtown to look over things before I head home to change. I'll be back here at 11:00 sharp."

Dale leaned and gave her fiancé' a quick kiss, "See that you do, and stay out of trouble. I'm looking forward to a pleasant time after yesterday's madness."

Giving Dale a quick smile, Doc was quickly out the door. Once in his roadster he turned to take the long way back to Swank Street through downtown. Saturday morning should be a busy time in the downtown shopping district. Most stores and many businesses were open for at least half the day and some all day long. Cruising through the streets Doc saw lots of activity; but little of it fit a normal Saturday.

Many stores were closed. Some owners were out boarding up broken windows or sweeping up debris on the sidewalks. There was a heavy police presence, as well as many Department of Sanitation personnel out cleaning up the littered streets. There were still more than a few damaged autos pushed to the curbs awaiting their turn to be towed away. All in all several blocks of downtown retail businesses had taken a beating. As he drove through the streets Doc could see no sign of the mysterious Blackness. He had thought there might be stains on the buildings or perhaps other signs that he might take a closer look at but he saw no signs of it. By the time he got back to his closed clinic he was totally puzzled. The Blackness had been real. He had seen it himself, but it had left no trace of its passing. He made a mental note to talk to Captain Griffin about this. Maybe Griffin had had the presence of mind to have his lab boys check for evidence; if there was any.

Inside his private apartment Doc found a note from Tommy stating he was going out to again search for information on the mysterious riot. Doc nodded and turned for his bedroom as he loosened his tie. He had time for a quick shower and change of clothes.

The day was hot and humid but the wind flowing over the open top of Doc Murdock's roadster created a pleasant breeze. It had also forced Dale to pull a scarf over her hair to keep it neatly in place as they drove.

The opening of the new Historical Society Museum was taking place at the recently refurbished Sykes mansion. This mansion was to the north of Akelton, a few miles out of town in an area of farms and open country. As Doc slowed his car to turn off the county road into the mansion's entrance he thought to himself that it wasn't all that far from the farm house where he had shot it out with Darnley's gang of jewel thieves last year. He smiled to himself as he drove past the brick gate posts and up the long graveled drive. Today was certainly going to be much more pleasant than that incident.

As they passed, Dale pointed out the brass plaque attached to one of the brick gate posts, "I remember coming out here with some of my high school girl friends when I was a girl. Everyone talked about the old Sykes place being haunted." She laughed as she pulled the scarf loose and shook her reddish-brown hair loose.

Doc replied, "Yeah, I came out here once when I was young too. I hear they've done a wonderful job restoring the old place. The new historical director is a wonderful fund raiser and organizer. He even talked me into making a donation to the restoration fund."

Dale looked surprised, "You've met him? What's he like?"

"Yes, I have. Um, he's coming up on middle age, balding. Seems likeable enough though, and he certainly knows his history. When I met him he nearly talked my leg off about Akelton history. I had to give him a donation in self-defense; otherwise I'd still be talking to him."

Dale laughed as they passed through some trees and their view opened up. Along both sides of the drive and in the grass nearby were parked dozens of automobiles. People were walking from the parked cars further up the drive to where some colorful tents could be seen along with even more people. The steep roofline and turret tops of a large building could be seen in the distance. Murdock pulled off the drive and found a place to park among the parked cars.

Once outside their car, Dale replaced the scarf with her new red hat. Doc nodded his approval, offered his arm to Dale and said, "I guess we follow the crowd." With Dale on his arm they walked a further hundred yards up to the large grassy area fronting the mansion. Doc had expected a good crowd and he wasn't disappointed. There was an open sided tent with tables and chairs inside and many people milling around. Dozens of men, women and couples strolled around the landscaped grounds. Many had drinks in their hands. Seeing this Dale squeezed Doc's arm, "It's so warm and muggy Miles, could you get me some lemonade?"

"Certainly, dear. I'll be right back." Doc released Dale's hand and quickly ducked into the open sided tent. There was plenty of food being served buffet style from the tables as well as bowls of punch and lemonade. There was also a bar doing a good business from all the suited dignitaries crowded around it. Ignoring the bar Doc grabbed two glasses of lemonade before returning to Dale. She had moved into the shade of a large oak tree and was fanning herself with a small folder.

Doc handed her the lemonade and took the folder from her, "What's this?"

"Oh, one of the passing waiters gave it to me. It's a brochure about the mansion and its history."

Doc sipped his lemonade as he glanced through the folded brochure. The Sykes mansion had been built by Albert Sykes in 1911. He had been a wealthy New Englander who had moved his family to Akelton. He had established several businesses and factories in town and been responsible for some of its early industrialization. He had had some business reversals around the time his wife died and was eventually forced to file for bankruptcy in 1924. He had committed suicide soon after. His mansion had gone to the county for unpaid taxes and had sat empty for many years. Recently, the new head of Akelton's Historical Society had engineered a public campaign to restore the mansion and make it a centerpiece of the Society as well as a museum of local Akelton history.

As he finished reading the brochure Dale remarked, "They have done a remarkable job on the old place. It looks as if it was built yesterday."

Looking up, Doc could only agree. The huge, stately, three story Victorian style mansion dominated a large piece of open ground in the middle of several landscaped acres, surrounded by forest. Decades old trees and many bushes had been carefully trimmed. Among them ran gravel pathways. A gravel drive ran to a large covered portico at the front of the mansion and around to a large carriage house along with several outbuildings located near the mansion.

The mansion itself was a classic example of Victorian architecture. There was not one but two round turrets set at the front corners of the building and the steep roof was adorned with several spires. Several of the second story windows actually had French doors leading to small balconies. It had an irregular skyline with several different roof areas and what appeared to Doc's eye to be a classic widow's walk high in the air above some third floor windows.

"It certainly looks like my donation has been well spent. I wonder if the inside is as impressive as the outside."

"The brochure says there'll be tours." Dale noted.

"Good. I'd like to see inside. But first I suppose we'd better mingle. The mayor said he wanted to thank me in person today." Doc took Dale's hand and they moved toward the largest knot of people gathered in and around another open sided tent. As they moved through the well-dressed crowd he recognized more than a few people. Doc Miles was well known and respected in Akelton; not only for his surgical reputation but for his charitable contributions and public profile. Doc served on several charitable boards and committees. As the couple strolled, Doc acknowledged former patients, acquaintances and fellow physicians. He had shaken plenty of hands and was wishing he had another glass of lemonade when he spied the Mayor nearby.

"There's the Mayor now," Doc pointed toward a knot of men standing close together. He guided Dale in their direction.

The Mayor was standing together with four overdressed men. Doc recognized them as Akelton's city council. They were smiling for a couple of professional photographers who were taking their photos. Leave it to politicians to find a photographer thought Doc as they neared the group.

Photos taken, the group broke up. One of the councilmen saw Murdock and came their way with his hand out and a smile on his face. This was the youngest councilman, Alan Paley who was running an active campaign in this year's election against Mayor Morningham. He was in his early thirties with dark hair and a winning smile. He had only moved to Akelton a few years before. He seemed to have money and had easily outspent his rival in winning a council seat two years before.

He approached and shook Doc's hand, "Dr. Murdock, it's a pleasure to see you here today." He turned to Dale and held out his hand, "I'm Alan Paley, we haven't met Miss . . ." As he spoke he gave Dale an appraising glance ending with a lingering look at her engagement ring. Doc had heard that Paley was a ladies man and he could see why given his smooth manner. He spoke up, "Let me introduce Miss Dale Jordan, my fiancée."

"It's a pleasure to meet you, Miss Jordan." Dropping her hand he turned smilingly to Doc, "I know you're a backer of the Mayor, but I look forward to talking with you about some of my ideas for Akelton."

Doc nodded diplomatically, "I look forward to that. I'm surprised to see you here today. I didn't think this gathering was to be political."

"Oh, it's not. I'm here in my official capacity. The entire council was invited for the ribbon cutting ceremony; although his honor will do the actual honors. Which reminds me; I have to go and find the fancy scissors. Can you believe that somebody actually painted them gold for the occasion? Please excuse me, doctor. Miss Jordan it was a pleasure meeting you."

"The pleasure was mine, Mr. Paley." Paley waved as he moved off through the crowd. "Well, he's certainly a charmer. I wouldn't be surprised if he gets more than a few votes," Dale speculated.

"Especially from the ladies," Doc commented wryly. Dale just laughed.

Councilman Ross; a thin, fortyish, man with thinning brown hair passed right by them. Ross was running a low-key campaign for Mayor as well. Doc wondered why he was putting so little effort into a campaign if he was interested in the position. He nodded to Doc as he passed, "Good to see you, Doctor."

"And you councilman," Doc responded.

The Mayor was now talking to a dapperly dressed, middle aged man with a cane as Doc and Dale came up. Several other people were listening as the mayor spoke cheerfully. Spying Doc the Mayor waved, "Miles, I'm glad you're here. Come and meet our host." As Doc and Dale moved forward the Mayor continued, "Elliot, may I introduce Dr. Miles Murdock and his lovely fiancée Dale Jordan. Miles, Dale, I'd like you to meet Dr. Elliot Sanderson, director of the Akelton Historical Society and our host today."

Doc held out his hand, "I've already had the pleasure, your Honor. It's good to see you again Dr. Sanderson."

Sanderson shook Doc's hand and smiled, "It's good to see you again, Dr. Murdock. I've enjoyed our chats and I have to thank you for your generosity in donating to the museum restoration." He was a middle aged man of middle height, his brown hair receding high up his forehead. Doc's guessed he was on the wrong side of forty at least. Although he leaned on a cane his right hand had a strong grip and his eyes were bright behind his metal rimmed glasses as he shook Doc's hand.

"You're very welcome Dr. Sanderson."

"Please, call me Elliot. It is a pleasure, Miss Jordan. May I say that Dr. Murdock is a most fortunate man," Sanderson said this last as he bowed slightly over Dale's hand.

Dale colored slightly as she replied, "Why thank you …Elliot."

Doc nodded toward the imposing building behind them. "It certainly looks like my money has gone to a good cause. You've done a remarkable job in restoring the property."

Sanderson turned and looked at the building, "The old Sykes place was a beautiful property in its day. I just hope we've managed to restore some of its former glory."

Dale put in, "You certainly have, Elliot."

He smiled courteously, "Why thank you Miss Jordan. I'm sure a woman can appreciate beautiful things. I hope you enjoy the interior as well. We've gone to great lengths using old photographs to restore much of the interior just as it was twenty years ago. Upstairs we've created a gallery with many photos and exhibits of local history"

Just then a stout, blonde haired, middle aged man walked up and whispered in the Mayor's ear. Doc recognized him as Richard Chapman another city councilman. The Mayor nodded and smiled at the group, "Excuse me, I have to greet some contributors." He allowed Chapman to pull him off toward another group of people. Dale then whispered to Doc, "It's hot out here. I need some more lemonade." She moved off toward an open sided tent where refreshments were available. That left Doc with Sanderson and the final councilman Henry MacPherson. Macpherson was fiftyish with a "lean hungry" look. He was well off financially, an ex-businessman who Doc didn't particularly care for. Doc thought he had taken a seat on the council just so he could advance his financial interests. Macpherson looked at Doc and asked, "You're backing the Mayor, aren't you Doctor?"

As Doc nodded, he could see Sanderson watching him closely. Was the historian interested in politics? Everyone else seemed to be. "Yes, I think the Mayor's done a good job the last few years. I don't see why he doesn't deserve another term."

Before Macpherson could reply Sanderson put in, "I think the Mayor has done a lot for this town. He has certainly endorsed the society's agenda to preserve Akelton's heritage."

Doc nodded, "I agree, Dr. Sanderson. Did the mayor have a hand in hiring you?"

Sanderson smiled, "I couldn't say. But the Mayor does sit on the Society's board of directors. They're the ones that hired me."

Doc was interested, "Where did you live before you came here doctor?"

"I was a history professor at a college in Georgia."

"Ah, I should have expected you would have an academic background." Doc turned back to Macpherson, "What do you think . . ." His question was cut off by a woman's scream. Doc spun around. From around the side of the tent where Dale had gone trotted three roughly dressed men wearing black hoods and carrying clubs. As Doc watched, one of them struck down a man standing in his way while another shoved a woman to the ground.

Doc immediately sprinted toward the third man now running in his direction. As the two reached each other Murdock ducked under the swing of the man's club and rammed a shoulder into his mid-section. The man's breath exploded from his lungs with a gasp, and he staggered back trying to keep his feet. Doc then ran toward the tent frantically looking for Dale. As he ran, chaos descended around him. He could hear shouts, curses and screams all around. People who minutes before were enjoying the warm day were now running in all directions. Doc fought himself through a crowd of people streaming away from the refreshment tent and suddenly found himself facing another hooded intruder bringing a club down on a defenseless man. Doc stepped in and grabbed the descending arm. He then threw a straight right punch into the hooded face. The intruder staggered back and as Doc stepped in, the man swung his club backhanded at the angry physician. Doc blocked the blow with his right forearm which immediately went numb from the terrific impact. He then fired in a straight left jab to the hooded face that sent the man sprawling.

Doc looked around. Where he had stood moment's ago he saw Councilman MacPherson on the ground and being beaten by two hooded attackers. As he watched, the limping Dr. Sanderson waded in and hit one of the attackers over the shoulders with his cane. The hooded man spun round, struck the cane out of the historian's hand and knocked him onto his back with a second blow of his club.

Murdock was torn. He wanted to go to the aid of the two men but he needed to find Dale. Shaking his head he jumped over his hooded opponent who was getting to his knees and ducked into the tent yelling, "Dale!"

All he could see were overturned tables and chairs. Two men lay on the ground groaning in pain. Then from under a table cloth covered table he saw Dale's head appear, "Miles, I'm here." Relieved Doc raced to her side, pulled her from under the table and hugged her, "Am I glad to see you."

"Oh, Miles! Those terrible men; where did they come from?" His arm around her Doc led her from under the tent, "Don't worry about them. Let's get you to safety." As soon as they reached sunlight they both stopped dead in their tracks. A wall of Blackness was moving across the grounds, blotting out the mansion as it rose into the bright sky. Dale gasped out, "Oh no! It's happening again!"

Doc swung her around and they both ran the other way. People were still running panicked in every direction. He caught sight of Sanderson getting to his feet holding a hand to his face. He also caught sight of Councilman Paley shoving through the crowd a panicked look on his face. The sight of the Blackness rolling across the grounds made the panic worse. Doc led the way toward the parked cars but they were slowed when they stopped to help a man to his feet whose face was covered in blood. Doc grabbed one of the groaning man's arms and led him along with Dale. They had made it to the nearest of the cars parked along the drive when the Blackness washed over them.

It was like being covered by a thick tarp. The Blackness was total. Doc Murdock could not see a thing; not even his hand when he raised it front of his face. It was definitely not smoke. As Dale had said he could breathe quite normally. If anything the air felt heavy and damp. Of course, the high humidity they were suffering through made every day feel damp and muggy. He could hear Dale nearby comforting the injured man. Elsewhere in the Blackness he could hear others shouting or screaming for help. His fists clenched in anger as he thought of the senseless violence. What was behind it? Who was behind it? His thoughts were interrupted by Dale calling out, "Miles, do you have a handkerchief?"

"Of course, just keep talking." Doc pulled his handkerchief out and moved carefully along the body of the auto he was next to toward the sound of Dale's voice. He found her and passed his handkerchief to her, "How is he?"

"He's got a head wound and he's stunned…a concussion, I think."

"Hold on. Help must be coming. The police should be here soon and I pray someone has called for ambulances. Here, let me check on him." Doc dropped to one knee to help Dale. There was not much he could do in the Blackness except check the man's pulse and breathing but it kept him busy and his anger in check. He felt his growing sense of helplessness as more screams and calls for help came from the Blackness. Minutes later the sounds of sirens cut through the chaos around them. Dale muttered, "Thank God." Doc stood up as a siren approached although he could not see it. It was then he realized the Blackness was receding. Visibility was increasing as the Blackness seemed to melt away. He barely made out the form of a police car push past him slowly, its siren still sounding. He turned and bent down next to Dale, "I think the worst is over."

He could barely see her face turned to him as she replied solemnly, "For now."

CHAPTER THREE

The Blackness faded away quickly once it started; something Murdock took close note of. As visibility returned to normal Doc could see that the grounds of the new Museum looked like a battlefield. Chairs and tables were overturned or smashed, tents were ripped down and stunned people wandered aimlessly amidst the debris. Discarded clothing, paper plates and other debris were scattered about the grounds. Injured people lay or sat in the grass looking dazed. It was perhaps twenty minutes since the attack had begun. There were dozens of police present now as well as ambulances and attendants. There was no sign of their hooded attackers. With visibility restored Doc and Dale pitched in to help the wounded. Most of the injuries were blunt trauma from fists and clubs. Not a few people had been trampled in the panic.

Dan Griffin found them minutes later. Doc was wiping blood off his hands with some colorful picnic napkins he had found. Dale was talking to an ambulance attendant. Griffin ran up to Doc and grabbed his elbow, "Doc, are you alright?"

"I'm fine. I wish I could say the same about a lot of these people." He waved his hand toward a group of injured lying on the ground awaiting their turn to be loaded in one of the waiting ambulances. Griffin looked grim, "What happened? Did you get a look at any of the attackers?"

"Not really. They all wore black hoods. I can tell you this though, they were incredibly violent. There whole purpose seemed to be to terrorize people."

Griffin nodded grimly, "I can see that. It's worse though; they kidnapped Henry MacPherson."

Surprised, Doc blurted, "What? Anyone else taken?"

"No, just MacPherson."

Doc looked thoughtful, "The Mayor was here; so was the rest of the city council and a lot of other important people too. Why would they want just Macpherson."

Griffin, "You got me, Doc. He isn't even running for Mayor."

At this comment Doc looked sharply at his friend. Something about what he had said struck a chord within him. Griffin continued, "Thank God you and Dale are alright." He lowered his voice, "Are you two headed straight home now?"

"I'm going to see Dale safe…then I've got work to do."

"What? Anyone else?"

Griffin nodded, "Take care, Doc." He then marched away calling for one of his officers. Minutes later Doc had pried Dale away from the wounded and bundled her into his car. The trip back to town was silent until Dale burst out, "That's two days in a row I've been swept up in a riot. I'm getting very tired of this and I think somebody better do something about it."

Doc was sympathetic, "I'm going to be working on it. I'm sorry that your day was ruined, dear. Let's head back to Swank Street and get cleaned up."

The drive back into the city was uneventful and soon they were entering Doc's quarters above his clinic. Tommy was impatiently waiting for their return.

"Hey, Doc. How was the party?"

"I'm afraid it was anything but a party." Doc quickly filled in his assistant as to the day's events. Tommy was nonplused but recovered quickly, "These guys are getting serious. But I got a line on them…maybe."

Interested Doc listened as Tommy related a story he had heard about street criminals being urged to gather downtown on Friday night. When Tommy was finished Doc asked, "Who did you hear this from?"

"His name was Jake. I'm not sure what his last name is. I heard him talking at a pool hall over on Tenth Street. He's a pickpocket and sneak thief. I've seen him around before. I don't know where he flops but I know where he likes to drink."

"Good, we're going to pay this Jake a visit tonight." They quickly made plans. When he left Tommy was smiling. Doc then turned to Dale, "These hooded men must have an agenda. The question is what? Do you think you can make a few calls this afternoon and find out if Darlan and MacPherson have any ties to each other?"

"I certainly can. I'm glad to help. If you don't figure this thing out soon, there's no telling what kind of riot I'm likely to get caught in the middle of tomorrow."

Miles Murdock smiled grimly.

CHAPTER FOUR

Sometime after ten o'clock that night the Purple Scar left Swank Street by the back alley. He was wearing a cheap, dark colored suit and carrying his usual assortment of gear. He was also wearing a newly made mask that carried the hardened face of a tough guy authentic down to a carefully molded broken nose that Doc was very proud of. The Purple Scar motored across town and parked in an alley off a rundown street populated by bars, pool halls and other less reputable establishments. Once away from his car the disguised avenger swaggered down the street. He looked around casually and then entered the *Getaway Bar*. On Saturday night the smoky interior was as busy as one would expect. The Scar pushed his way through the crowds looking for familiar faces. There; at the end of the bar facing the door sat Tommy drinking a beer. Shouldering his way in next to his aide the Scar gave a concealed nudge to the little man. He then yelled out for some service.

Soon enough the bar tender came and took the Scar's order. A beer in hand the masked man drank thirstily. Tommy seeing that no one was paying any attention to the two interlopers whispered quietly, "He was here earlier. I followed him home. I'm sure he's in for the night." The Scar ignored him and took another drink of his beer. Eventually he glanced casually around the bar. Minutes later he finished his beer, tossed some coins on the bar, turned and slouched toward the front entrance.

Soon Tommy exited the bar and looked around. The Purple Scar stepped out of a doorway, waved and then turned for his car. Moments later Tommy joined him in the roadster. He started the car and drove away. Tommy quietly directed them several blocks away to a street of walk up boarding houses and of cheap brownstone apartments.

The Scar parked around the corner on a dark side street. The nearest street light was out of commission and with the top up the roadster was very dark inside. Tommy kept watch outside as the Scar exchanged his tough guy mask for the horrid featured purple mask he pulled from its hidden pocket. When he had re-masked he turned to Tommy and said, "Lead the way." The two men got out of the car and walked around the corner. Halfway down the block Tommy led the way up the four steps to the stoop of a brownstone. The outer door was locked but the Scar's master keys made short work of the simple lock. Inside Tommy led the way up the stairs. At the third floor landing he whispered, "Our man is in #33; halfway down the hall on the right."

The Purple Scar whispered back, "Wait for me in the car. This shouldn't take long." Tommy nodded his agreement and disappeared back down the stairway. The lock of #33 yielded to the second key he tried and the Scar silently slipped into the darkened apartment and closed the door behind him.

Inside the Scar pulled his revolver out with his right hand and his pencil flash with left. A quick flash of his light showed a combination living room and a kitchen. Two doors opened to his left. He crept to the half open one and pushed it open. It squeaked slightly to reveal a rather unsavory bathroom. He moved quickly to the door furthest from the hall. After listening for a moment he turned the knob and pushed the door open. It swung wide with only the slightest of squeaks. The bedroom was very dark, illuminated only by dim starlight filtering through thin curtains at the window. Snoring came from the shadowy figure occupying a narrow bed. Taking in the situation the vigilante pocketed his flash and stepped across to the window and threw up the sash. Warm, humid air wafted inward. Turning, he bent over the sleeping figure and dragged him up and out of the sagging bed.

Half-awake the startled man struggled, "Hey! Who the hell . . ." His voice cut out as the Scar slammed him hard against the wall next to the window. The man's head bounced off the flaking plaster and his jaw banged closed painfully on his tongue. The man hissed with pain and attempted to curse but when his mouth opened the Purple Scar shoved the barrel of his revolver into it. The man froze his eyes wide. The Scar leaned in close enough for the frightened man to recognize his horrible features before hissing, "Do you know who I am?"

Wide awake now, the frightened man nodded, the Scar's revolver scraping at his teeth. With his free hand the masked man wrapped his gloved fingers around the man's throat and hissed, "I'm going to ask you some questions and I want answers, understand?"

The man known as Jake nodded again. The Scar pulled his gun back and holstered it. His victim let out a breath reeking of stale beer. The Scar then whispered harshly, "I want to know what you know about last night's riot."

Jake's mouth opened and stuttered, "Uh, I dunno wha—" His voice cut off as the gloved hand squeezed his neck. He scrabbled with his hands at the arm encircling his throat but the Scar just squeezed harder. After a few moments of this the masked avenger grew impatient. He let go of the Jake's throat and spun him around smacking his face hard against the wall. Then he bent one of the man's arms around behind his back and grabbing him by the scruff of the neck he thrust Jake's upper body out the window.

"Nooooo," Jake yelled! He scrabbled with his free hand at the window's edge for a grip to save himself as the Purple Scar grated in his ear, "Someone told you to go downtown last night in time for the riot. Tell me what you know!"

Jake half sobbed, "Okay! Okay, I'll talk!" He paused and gulped for air before his words began tumbling out. "We was shootin' pool over at *McGuire's* Wednesday night when these two mugs come in. It was kinda quiet and me and a couple the guys was the only ones shootin.' So these two look around and one of 'em comes over and starts talkin' . . ."

What was his name?"

"He didn't say. He just starts askin' if we was interested in some easy money."

"What did he look like?"

"Uh, he was kinda skinny with red hair."

"Then what?'

"Like I say. He says that if we're looking for an easy score we should hang around downtown Friday along about sunset. We asked what was up but he just said to bring our friends, that there would be some easy money to be had."

The Scar thought for a moment before snarling, "So you took his advice?" This question was accompanied by a further shove on Jake's back. The thief scrabbled at the window frame and squeaked, "Yeah! Yeah! But as soon as the trouble started I ran. I didn't want to have anything to do with all that stuff, especially those guys in the black hoods."

Interested now, the Scar leaned his fearsome visage in next to Jake's face and whispered, "Tell me about them!"

"Uh, I don't know nothin' I just saw some of 'em before that black fog stuff rolled in. I didn't like the look of 'em though."

"How many did you see? And what were they doing?"

"Uh, they was sneaking out of an alley. I da' know what they was up to but it couldn't of been good…and I didn't wanna have nothin' to do with no fire."

"What do you mean?" hissed the figure tightening the hold on Jake's neck.

"Well, one of them guys had one of those flame thrower things, like you see in the news reels."

Taken by surprise the Scar thought furiously, "Are you sure? What did it look like?"

"Uh, there was a thing on his back…like a tank or somethin' and the mug was holding some kind of hose that ran from it. It looked just like what I seen at the movies."

Surprised, the Purple Scar shook the little man, "And, that's all you know?"

"Honest, Scar! I'm tellin' you everything!"

"What else do you know about the men at the pool hall?"

"Nothin," he hesitated. "Just that they was furriners."

The Scar frowned under his fearsome mask, "Foreigners?"

"Yeah, the carrot top talked like he was Irish or maybe Scotch."

"He had an accent?"

"Yeah, and the other one too."

"He was Irish too?"

"Naw, he had black hair he looked like he was Mexican or somethin."

"Did he say anything?"

"Naw, but I heard him whispering with the Mick. It sounded like Spanish or somethin' like that."

The Scar paused for a second to absorb this new information. Jake took that moment to whine, "Please, Mister! Lemme back in."

A stronger squeeze to the back of Jake's neck accompanied the next question, "And that's all you know?"

"Honest, that's all I know," he sniveled. The Scar could feel the man shaking even in the warm night air. He jerked Jake backwards, banging the rear of his head on the open sash. He then threw the man violently to the floor. Bending over the shivering man the Purple Scar whispered harshly, "If you're lying...I'll be back! I know where to find you."

Turning he left without another word. In the hall he walked quickly toward the stairwell. Down the stairs and out through the front hall he went. As the Scar opened the front door onto the darkened street he stopped. Four steps below him on the sidewalk, a late night passerby had stopped to light a cigarette. Startled by the sound of the door opening just eight feet away the man turned with a jerk and stared up at the figure standing in the door of the brownstone. The nearest streetlight was twenty yards away but enough light fell on the Scar's face to clearly show his horribly disfiguring features. The cigarette fell from the lips of the startled man. He backed away until he stepped off the sidewalk into the deserted street. He almost fell but caught himself, turned and fled down the street as fast as he could run.

Moments later, Doc Murdock stepped into the roadster as Tommy started the engine. Once they were moving the Scar peeled off his mask and stuffed it back into his jacket. As he did he related his conversation with hapless Jake. As he steered through the darkened streets Tommy asked, "Whatta ya think, Boss?"

Doc was thoughtful in his reply, "I'm not sure. No one seems to know anything. Maybe that means there's a new gang in town no one's ever heard of. If so; they're exceptionally organized." There was a thoughtful pause, "I didn't like what Jake said about a flame thrower. Where would a gang of hoods get something like that? And if they have it why didn't they use it? Jake also said he thought the men who talked to him were foreign. That's very interesting." Doc fell silent for a moment, "But why is this gang kidnapping people? Are they're targeting specific men?" Tommy had no reply to that. Doc was silent for the remainder of the trip back to Swank Street, his mind racing over possibilities.

CHAPTER FIVE

The next morning Murdock skipped breakfast. Instead he pored over the morning newspaper with just a cup of coffee for company. In the background a radio was tuned to a local station for the news; which was all bad. The biggest newspaper headlines were, of course, about the attack on the Museum opening. They were certainly not flattering toward the authorities. Other articles concerned several "smash and grab" type robberies that had happened around the city the night before. The articles speculated about a link between the rash of robberies, the black hooded men and the frightening Blackness.

Most troubling to Doc's way of thinking was an editorial in the newspaper. It took the current city administration to task for a lack of response to this new series of crimes. It was especially critical of the Mayor's leadership. He found it annoying that John Landau the publisher of Akelton's largest daily newspaper would use these crimes to increase readership. Or was there more to it than that? Was it political? Why else turn his editor Wells loose? Wells wouldn't start a crusade without tacit agreement of his publisher. Even worse was a letter to the editor from Councilman Paley calling for a stronger police response. Doc grimaced; the candidate certainly hadn't waited long to make political points off the current crisis.

Doc folded the paper closed on the editorial page and thought for a moment. Perhaps there was a political motive behind the Blackness and the hooded men. At that point he was distracted by a news bulletin on the radio. The announcer was saying that the body of George Darlan had been found early that morning. His cause of death was unknown but the police were investigating.

Doc turned off the radio and crossed through his apartment to his study. Grabbing up the telephone he dialed police headquarters. Soon he was connected to Dan Griffin.

"Hello Miles, what can I do for you?" Doc could hear the strain in Griffin's voice. He spoke carefully, "I heard that you found George Darlan's body this morning."

"Yes, a beat officer found the body dumped on the steps of one of Darlan's businesses. No sign of any one around. He must have been dumped there very late last night."

"What was the cause of death?"

Griffin sighed, "We won't know for sure until the autopsy but it looks like he was beaten to death. The body was in pretty bad shape."

"Any other news about yesterday?"

"Not a thing. Lots of witnesses but not much accurate detail…but you were there you saw how chaotic it was. Other than the hooded men, what did you see once the Blackness rolled in? Nothing, right? It's the same with all the witnesses, including the Mayor. What the heck is that stuff, Miles? It's spooking everybody, including some of my men."

"Whatever it is, the hooded men seem to command it. I found a person who was downtown Friday night and saw some of these hooded men just before the Blackness rolled in."

"Well, we'd better find a way to combat it…"

"…Before the next incident" Doc finished.

Griffin agreed and ended the conversation. After Murdock hung up he went down stairs to his clinic office to catch up on paperwork. By noon his desk was tidy. He was reaching for the telephone when it rang. He answered, "Hello."

"Doc? It's me." Tommy's voice came over the line.

"Tommy, are you alright?"

"Sure, Doc. I called to tell you I heard some more rumors and I'm going to check up on them tonight."

"Good. Where shall I meet you?"

"Uh, I'm not sure that's a good idea. The guys I'm meeting are kind of harmless and they might not take well to uh…you know, uh rough stuff."

Doc smiled to himself, "I understand. As long as you'll be alright."

"Oh sure, I'll be fine. I'll talk to you tomorrow."

"Good luck."

"Thanks' Doc."

After he had hung up, Murdock quickly dialed again. Within seconds Dale answered, "Hello."

"Dale, I thought I'd call and see if you've heard anything."

"Actually, I have Miles. I've called a few friends. Everyone seems to think that Darlan and MacPherson knew each other socially but aren't active friends. Although one lady I know is sure that they had business dealings a long time ago."

"That's a start Dale. We'll do more tomorrow, but we still have patients to see."

"I'll be at the clinic bright and early tomorrow. Until then I'll make a few more calls. Uh, what are you doing?"

"Well, I think the Purple Scar needs to be out on the streets tonight keeping an eye on things."

There was a pause, "Well, tell him to be careful if you see him."

"I will." After the conversation was over, Doc thought for a moment before heading for his studio; time to check his masks.

CHAPTER SIX

Monday was busy at the Down Street free clinic Doctor Murdock operated. He had no surgeries scheduled but there were several consultations and follow up exams. The only time Doc took for himself was when Captain Griffin came calling. In Doc's office the square jawed detective expressed his frustration, "We're getting a lot of pressure downtown, Miles."

"And no new clues?"

"Nothing. There have been several sightings of hooded men but we don't know if it's the same group. Some hooded men smashed up a jewelry store last night but it seemed more like an ordinary robbery than one of these new crimes, and there was no sign of the Blackness. There's been a lot of street crime like that the last couple of days."

"Do you think some of the gangs are taking advantage of the confusion for their own gain?"

"I'm sure of it. The question is who and how much? Unfortunately the source of trouble no longer matters. The public is worried. The Mayor is under a lot of pressure and he's passing it down to us. The Chief is treading on our coat tails to get some results. Have you heard anything at all?"

"Just that last Friday was even more orchestrated than we thought. In the days before the riot, people were going around to the local haunts telling people to congregate downtown. For some the lure was jobs, for others the lure was for quick money. Just last night Tommy tracked down some out of work men living down by the tracks. They claim a man came around last week telling them to be downtown Friday night for free food and clothing."

Griffin looked thoughtful, "That's interesting."

"Yes, it looks like someone wanted large crowds downtown to witness and amplify the chaos he or she was about to create. The most interesting thing is these supposed organizers may have been foreign."

"Really?"

"Yes, it seems that some of these organizers had foreign accents. Tommy says a couple of men last night claimed the man who spoke to them sounded Irish. And while I was out last night keeping my ears open I heard others talk of dark haired men with accents also."

"So you suspect foreign agents?"

"Maybe; maybe this whole thing is political. There is an election soon and the Mayor is getting a lot of criticism. Have you seen the papers this morning?" Murdock had quickly scanned the newspaper before work. It was the same as the day before. Attention grabbing headlines about crimes were front and center. There were plenty of letters to the editor and guest editorials as well.

Griffin nodded grimly, "I've seen them. People are scared. There's an emergency meeting of the city Council tonight. Councilman Paley is supporting a vote of no confidence against the Mayor. I also hear the governor is sending a representative to attend."

Doc smiled, "I plan to be there. Are you going to speak?"

"No, but the chief wants me there to answer questions, if needed. I'm not looking forward to it."

"I'm not either. But I want to be there to hear the opposition up close. You say that Paley is calling for a vote of no confidence in the Mayor? It's not a coincidence that Paley's running against him. Maybe he's just taking advantage of a bad situation and maybe there's more to it than that. It's troubling that this mayhem is hitting in the middle of a tough campaign. And with the political climate all across the country it may be outside agitators; Fascists or Communists trying to undermine our institutions."

Griffin looked even grimmer at Doc's suggestion, "I hope you're wrong Miles."

"So do I."

The rest of the day passed quickly. The main topic of conversation among his patients and staff was of course the black hooded men and the chaos they were causing. Doc heard nothing concrete but the rumors that were spreading were alarming. When they had seen the last patient out and the clinic locked securely Doc and Dale had a few minutes to themselves. As Doc changed his white coat for his suit jacket he said, "The city council meeting tonight is at 7:30. I'll be home after it's over. What do you have planned?"

"I'm meeting a friend. Then she's going to take me to meet Alice Kriegle."

Doc was surprised, "The widow Kriegle? The Doyenne of Akelton society?" The dowager widow Kriegle presided over Akelton's 'old money' social set. She was a direct descendent of General Alfred Kriegle one of the founders of Akelton in the last century.

"The very same. It seems the widow Kreigle is giving a small dinner for a few friends. My friend Betsy got us invitations. Betsy claims the old dame knows all the gossip on everyone who's anyone in town. I want to ask her about Darlan and MacPherson."

Doc nodded, "Good. Give me a call at home later and we'll compare notes. And, don't stay out too late. We have a busy day tomorrow at Down Street."

"I won't, and I'm sure I'll have plenty of gossip for you tomorrow."

CHAPTER SEVEN

Two hours later the disguised Purple Scar worked his way through the crowds entering City Hall. Instead of his worn gray suit he now wore a better cut suit and the face of an average looking, brown haired man. His fearsome purple mask resided in a hidden pocket of that suit as well as his usual tools of the trade. His revolver was holstered on his hip under the jacket.

Despite the evening hour, City Hall was crowded with people that night. The large, tall atrium was crowded with police, reporters, curious citizens and possibly even a few people who were actually there on legitimate business. The Scar worked his way through the crowd to the wide open stairs leading to the mezzanine level or what would be the third floor in any normal building. He crossed along the balcony overlooking the atrium and followed the crowd down a hallway filled with people. He soon reached the City Council room. The room was large but already it was crowded with anxious people. By the time the Scar arrived all the seats were taken and people were still crowding in. This suited the masked avenger. He took a place standing against the back wall near one of the doors. This way he could get a good look at the crowd. As he listened to quiet, and some not so quiet conversations, the disguised crime-fighter could feel the sense of fear floating through the room. The crowd was restless and the Scar did not envy the city officials who would be speaking.

Scanning the crowd he saw many familiar faces. It seemed like most of Akelton's important movers and shakers were present. He caught sight of Elliot Sanderson sitting next to Thomas Wells the editor of Akelton's largest newspaper. Wells was busy scribbling on a notepad. The Scar wondered to himself if Wells was outlining his next critical editorial or if he was interviewing Sanderson about his attempted heroics at Saturday's chaos.

Finally the Mayor and councilmen filed in from another door and took their places at the long table running along the rear of the chamber. Conversations faded as The Mayor opened the proceedings with a short upbeat talk and then turned floor over to the Chief of Police Charles Baxter. The chief was standing against one of the chamber's side walls along with several senior police officers, Griffin among them. They weren't the only police officers in the building. The Scar had been impressed by the number of officers posted at the doors to the building, stationed outside in the hallway or scattered through the building. Saturday's debacle was still fresh on everyone's mind. The chief's positively slanted speech didn't set many minds at ease. The building tension of the crowd could be felt.

Immediately after Chief Baxter had finished Councilman Paley took the floor. He immediately accused the Mayor of mishandling the crisis. This caused a stir in the crowd. He then practically accused the Mayor of incompetence. The Mayor's face flushed red and it was obvious he could barely contain himself. The Scar took note of the reporters crowded into the front row all scribbling furiously.

He turned his attention back to Paley just as the councilman demanded the Mayor ask for State Police to assist the local forces. This caused another stir in the crowd as Councilman Chapman interrupted in a loud voice. The mention of State Police gave the Scar a moment's pause. Was Akelton's finest being stretched too far? He glanced around at the uniformed officers in the room. They couldn't be everywhere at once and the hooded men could strike wherever they chose.

A sudden prickling came at the base of the disguised avenger's neck. This was just the sort of gathering that Akelton's unknown attackers had targeted on Saturday. Turning he slipped toward the rear doors as the

Mayor called for order. Once in the corridor he walked decisively toward the restroom at the end of the hall near the stairs. He took stock as he did. Everything seemed normal. The hallway was packed around the entrance to the council chamber as latecomers crowded around the door. There were two uniformed policemen in the hall.

Near the restroom the Scar looked around casually and then ducked into the rear stairwell instead of the restroom. He paused to listen. The stairwell was silent. He leaned over the hand rail and looked down but saw no one in the dim light. With the stairwell clear he slipped back into the hallway and quickly ducked around a corner. Walking briskly down this hallway he saw no one and heard no sounds other than the distant raised voices from the council chambers.

The Scar circled through the second floor halls and wound up back on the balcony overlooking the atrium and entry to City Hall. Nothing was amiss but he still felt a sense of danger nearby. Hands on the railing he was staring down toward the front entrance when there was a bright flash from somewhere outside in the street. The flash was accompanied by the BOOM! of a nearby explosion. The disguised hero turned and sprinted for the curving front stairs. He charged down the steps three at a time and dashed across the atrium reaching for his hip. Police officers were fighting their way through fleeing civilians toward the exit doors. Pushing through one of the glass doors he skidded to a stop at the top of the concrete steps.

There was panic on the brightly lit street. Screaming people were fleeing from the park across the street. A car screeched to a stop at the bottom of the stairs and gunfire erupted from the back seat. The Purple Scar threw himself sideways pulling a policeman to the ground with him as gunfire raked the front doors of City Hall. The machine gun cut a ragged path up the steps and across the front of the building shattering glass and sending chips of marble flying in all directions. He felt one shard slice across the back of his left hand.

The gunfire cut off abruptly and tires screeched as a car accelerated away. Scrambling to his feet the Scar leaped down the steps. There were curses and yells all around him. As he angled toward a body lying on the sidewalk he heard yells turning to screams; "Look!" The Blackness!" He looked across the street and sure enough a wall of the impenetrable Blackness was rolling out of the park and into the street.

The Scar saw the advancing Blackness and instantly recognized it for what it was. He cursed and turned to leap back up the steps two at a time. Pushing through the crowds of panicky people at the doors he reached the atrium. Ignoring the stairs he shoved his way through the crowd and reached the door to the rear stairwell moments later. Inside the stairwell he could hear muffled yells from the upper floors but the lobby landing was quiet. In the relative privacy of the dimly lit stairwell he pulled off his mask, stuffed it in his pocket and quickly replaced it with the fearsome purple mask that was the terror of Akelton's underworld. His pistol in his hand the Purple Scar ran up the stairs and threw his shoulder against the mezzanine level door. He spilled out into a hallway filled with noise. Confusion reigned. Twenty feet away the hallway leading to the council chambers was filled with Blackness. Screams and curses came from within it. As he watched a man staggered out of it holding a hand to his bloody head. With the impenetrable Blackness advancing toward him rapidly the Scar turned and ran down a corridor leading toward the rear of the building.

The explosion and shooting on the street had been a diversion, the Scar was certain of it. There had been no one on the stairs so they must be escaping out the rear. He rounded a corner and saw more darkness ahead. A short corridor leading toward the rear of the building was on his right. At the end of the hall an open window let in humid night air. Sprinting to the window he threw his leg over the window ledge and onto a fire escape landing. He ducked through and came up looking down at the dim alley behind City Hall.

Forty feet away to the left, two hooded men were shoving a man into the back seat of a dark colored, idling sedan. Another similar auto was parked right behind the first. Two more hooded men stood next to the rear of the second car. They were watching the window where the masked vigilante had appeared. As soon as they saw him they immediately opened fire with handguns. Bullets ricocheted off the metal fire escape framework as he ducked down and returned fire; Bang! Bang! The lead car chirped tires as it accelerated down the alley. He quickly threw two more slugs at the fleeing auto. As he did, the two hooded men jumped for the open doors of the second car. The Scar raised his revolver in both hands and sighting down the darkened alley carefully fired his last two shots. The hooded man rounding the rear of the auto was thrown violently against the trunk and then slid to the ground his pistol clattering away. Holstering his gun, the Scar ducked into the opening of the floor at his feet and got footing on the counter-weighted ladder. His weight triggered it and the ladder swung down to the alley floor with a clang. Grabbing the rails and clamping his shoes around the outside of the rails, he slid quickly to the alley floor. The second car was speeding down the alley; too far for a good shot even if his gun wasn't empty.

Instead the Scar reached for his pocket flash as he reached the fallen man. Kneeling down he flashed the light on as he pulled the hood from the man's face. He was dead of course, his sightless eyes staring upward. The man was of swarthy complexion with black hair and a thin mustache adorning his upper lip. He had the look of Latin or perhaps Mediterranean heritage. His clothes were rough workman's clothing with a leather jacket. A quick frisk of the man's pockets produced nothing but a spare magazine for the man's discarded .45 Colt.

Frustrated at not finding any identification at all, the Scar stood up. He looked up at the fire escape. Blackness shrouded the window and was billowing out into the alley. Distant shouts and sirens sounded from the other side of the building. Shaking his head he turned and jogged off down the alley: Another round to the unknown Master of Blackness.

It was hours before Miles Murdock reached home. Switching back to his innocent appearing mask the Scar had hung around the edges of the crowds at City Hall trying to pick up gossip and rumors until the police finally started clearing the crowd away. Because of the confusion downtown it took a while to get back to his roadster and return to Swank Street. As he emptied his pockets of his master keys, pencil flash and set his holstered revolver on his desk, the phone rang. It was Griffin, "Miles, you're finally home."

"Yes, I just got here. What's the news?"

"All bad, I'm afraid. Were you at the council meeting?"

"I was. Quite a show."

"Then you saw it all?"

"A bit of it; I take it the explosion across the street was a diversion?"

"Not exactly. It did cause confusion but it was the statue of General Templeton. It was dynamited. A swipe at the city's reputation, I guess."

Doc shook his head, "And the body in the street?"

There was a pause before Griffin continued in a tired voice, "Henry MacPherson, I'm afraid. He was beaten to death."

As Doc mulled this news over, Griffin continued, "There's something else...Morris Bannerman was kidnapped last night."

Recalling the previous evening, Doc said grimly, "I saw him at the Council meeting."

"That's right. He was taken in the confusion of the Blackness. We think he was spirited out through the back alley. Uh, we found the body of a hooded man shot to death in the alley. The Purple Scar wouldn't have been downtown last night, would he?"

"It's possible."

"I suppose it's too much to ask that he leave a wounded suspect to be questioned."

"I don't know since I wasn't there but it seems like these hooded men are pretty dangerous, Dan. It's kind of hard to take a prisoner when the man is shooting at you."

Griffin sighed heavily, "I suppose so. We're trying to identify the man but not having much luck so far."

"That may be difficult."

"I know. He was carrying absolutely nothing to identify him. No letters, not even a laundry mark on his clothes. Somebody really wanted to remain anonymous."

Doc arched an eyebrow as he thought that over, "Yes. He certainly did. Why do you think that is?"

"No idea, Miles. I'll let you know if we find out anything more." Doc thanked Griffin and hung up. No sooner had he set the phone down than it rang again. It was Dale, "Miles. Are you alright? I heard on the radio about tonight."

"I'm fine. But it was the Historical Society all over again. The same hooded men used their mysterious Blackness to break up the Council meeting and kidnap another man."

"Oh Miles, something's got to be done. This can't go on much longer."

"I agree. Did you find out anything?"

"A little bit, I think."

"Good, let's talk about it tomorrow at the clinic." Dale agreed and they said "Goodnight." After hanging up Doc went to his study. With all the lights off except a reading light on his desk, he sat there for a long time thinking. What was his next move? More importantly, what was his opponent's next move?

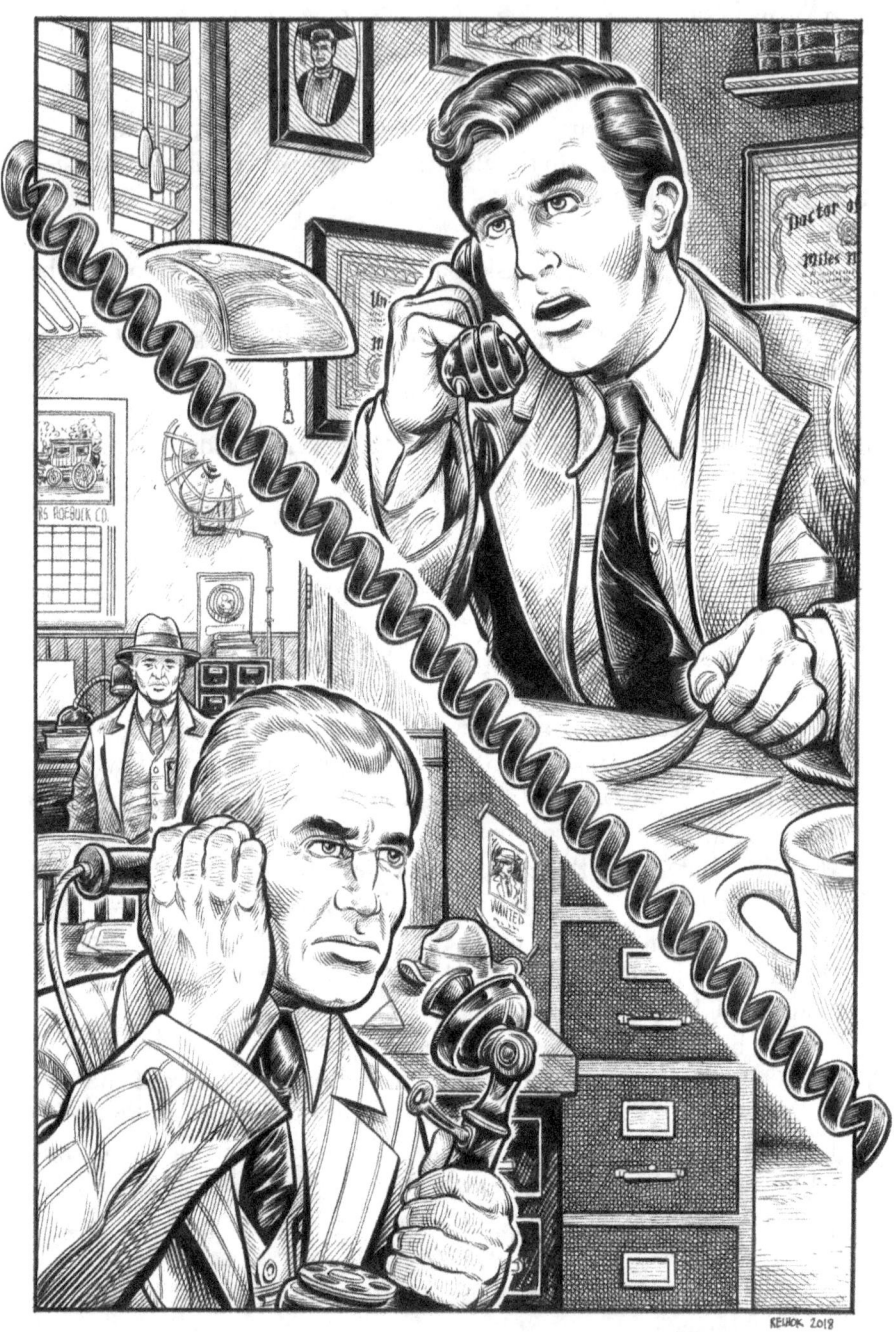

"We're trying to identify him…"

CHAPTER EIGHT

Dale arrived at the Down Street Clinic to find Miles already there. He was talking to Tommy. He handed an envelope to his aide and said, "I want you to go out and find us another car. My roadster is too well known. The Purple Scar has been using it too much. I think we need something a little less conspicuous."

Tommy nodded, "Right, something dependable but invisible."

Doc smiled, "Yes, something like that. Use that cash and put it in your name."

Tommy smiled at Dale and disappeared toward the back door. Doc turned to his fiancé' and smiled. She returned the smile and said, "Already busy this morning?"

"I'm afraid so. Dan just called. The interrupted Council meeting is to be re-convened this afternoon. I'll head down there after lunch. So, what did you find out from Mrs. Kriegle?"

Dale spoke as she adjusted her nurse's cap, "Well, it seems that Darlan and Macpherson are acquainted socially but interestingly they used to be much closer. Mrs. Kriegle said they used to be partners. I know it was a little before our time but you remember all the development that went on after the war, don't you?"

Doc had been a boy then but he did remember the whole country being in an exuberant mood. It's what had eventually led to the stock market speculation and eventually the Great Crash, "I remember a lot of businesses got started then and there was a lot of building going on in town."

"Right. Well, it seems like Darlan and Macpherson, along with a bunch of other rich men were right in the middle of all that. Mrs. Kriegle hinted that the two of them were in some pretty big deals back then."

Murdock asked, "Did they get hurt in the Crash of '29?"

"I guess not. Apparently, they weren't into stocks as much as development and real estate."

"Huh…Bannerman is a wealthy banker. I wonder if he had many dealings with Darlan and MacPherson?"

Dale pointed to the newspaper she had carried in, "I haven't read the paper yet. Is that who was kidnapped last night?"

Doc frowned, "Yes. I was right there and they still got away with it."

"Don't blame yourself, Miles. They had you outnumbered and they have that horrible…Blackness, or whatever it is."

Doc nodded. He would give a lot to know how these hooded men could command the Blackness. More importantly he needed to know what and who was behind these attacks. Looking again at Dale he said, "We'll close the clinic at noon. Why don't you go and see if you can connect Bannerman to the others. I'll meet you at your place this evening." Dale nodded her assent and the two prepared for their morning appointments.

CHAPTER NINE

After a quick lunch Miles Murdock made his way downtown to City Hall. He was forced to park a block away. The police were taking no chances after last night. The street in front of City Hall was closed to traffic and there were officers with riot guns patrolling the barricades. Doc walked closer hoping that his notoriety would get him through the check point. Around him he saw other prominent Akeltonians heading the same way. He was about seventy yards away from the entrance to City Hall when he skidded to a halt. Across the street a cloud of Blackness was again boiling up from the city park. Already it was expanding across the sidewalk toward the street. Doc broke into a run but again skidded to a halt as a scream came from behind him. He spun around. Three men in black hoods had spilled out of a narrow alley. All carried short clubs. The three had immediately launched themselves at a man walking down the sidewalk.

He cursed and sprinted toward the attack. The well-dressed man was down on the sidewalk trying to protect his head from the blows raining down on him when Murdock arrived. Remembering his old football days Doc stretched out and launched himself in a flying tackle at one of the attackers. The man crashed to the sidewalk with Doc on top of him. His club went flying as the two rolled apart. Doc scrambled to his feet and caught the hooded man with a right uppercut as he was climbing off his knees. The man flew backward landing with a breath shaking thud on his back. Movement caught out of the corner of his eye caused Murdock to duck as a club swished over his head. Turning he grabbed the descending club arm of his attacker. He then dropped his shoulder and threw a left handed punch that caught the hooded man in his side. He followed that with another that doubled the man forward. Doc grabbed the club in an attempt to wrench it away when something big and heavy exploded on his head. Lights flashed and for just a moment Doc actually saw stars before darkness descended on him.

Dan Griffin was in the atrium of City Hall giving orders to one of his officers when the first cries came from out in the street. He dashed for the front doors drawing his revolver as he ran. Bursting out on to the top of the stone steps he was not surprised to see a wave of Blackness pouring out of the park. His attention was immediately drawn to the sidewalk as two of his officers vaulted the barricades and ran down the street to the right yelling, "Stop! Police!" His gaze drawn that way Griffin saw two black hooded men loading a limp body into the back of a sedan. As the limp body rolled briefly toward him Griffin could have sworn that it looked just like Miles Murdock. Ignoring the commands of his men the kidnappers jumped into the car after their victim and it screeched away down the street.

Grimly Griffin commanded the officers near him to retreat into the building and lock the doors after them. A kidnapping had happened in front of his eyes but the Captain's first duty was to protect City Hall from another attack. Miles, if that was who the unconscious man was, would have to look after himself for the time being.

Doc gradually became aware of his surroundings. He knew he had been knocked unconscious. The blow must have been severe because he could feel the earth heaving and rolling beneath him. His head was throbbing and he could not see anything. Blood in his eyes, perhaps? He was very tired and wanted nothing more than to drift off and rest for a few moments and that's just what he did.

Doc was wrenched back to consciousness as he bounced off something hard and slammed back down on his face. It was then he realized that the rolling sensation he felt earlier came not from his head but from the rumbling vehicle he was in, jolting down a rough road. Fighting past the pain in his head, Murdock took stock. He could not see because his head was covered by rough cloth. His mouth was gagged and his mouth felt foul and oily, probably from the cloth stuffed in it to gag him. His hands were also tied behind him.

His head was throbbing but his thoughts were clearing and he soon realized he was face down in the back of a large truck. He could feel the rough boards of the truck bed under him. Every time the truck hit a rut in whatever poor road it was traveling on he was jarred up and down or side to side. Doc was tempted to try and brace himself from this jolting but quickly decided that it might be in his interest to seem as if he was still unconscious.

Soon Doc felt something roll over against his legs. It was soft and heavy and it did not move. Quickly he decided it was another body. Was it the unfortunate man he had tried to help? Possibly. Murdock was furious with himself. He had been caught unawares by the brazen daylight attack. He had blindly thrown himself at the attackers instead of fighting more cautiously. There were police nearby. If he could have just slowed the attackers instead of trying to knock them all out singlehandedly he probably wouldn't be trussed up like a Thanksgiving turkey headed for God knows where.

The truck ride went on for some time. It made several turns on what Doc guessed were dirt or gravel roads from their roughness. Eventually the truck slowed and made a sharp turn before proceeding at a slower pace. Soon it slowed to a halt and a door slammed. Doc sensed movement around him and he was picked up by at least two men and handed down out of the truck. Out of the truck he knew he was in the open from warm sunshine striking the burlap sack pulled over his head. He heard soft grunted commands in a foreign language. He was carried out of the sun and into cooler shade for a distance before the men carrying him stopped. He heard them discuss something in what he was sure was Spanish. He was then carried through a doorway into a darkened room and dropped carelessly onto a hard concrete floor. His breath was knocked from him momentarily by the impact. By the time he recovered, the men had slammed a door closed. Doc Murdock heard a lock turn and he was left in darkness and silence.

+++

Answering the knock at her apartment door, Dale swung it open to find a nervous looking Tommy Pedlar standing in the hall his hands nervously twisting his cap, "Is it true?"

Trying to look brave Dale stood aside and waved him inside, "I'm afraid so. Dan Griffin called an hour ago. How did you hear about it?"

"It was on the radio. They was saying how the black hoods had struck again; kidnapping two men right in front of City Hall. They said the men were identified as guy named Russo and Dr. Murdock. What are we gonna do?"

Dale walked into the kitchen and started making coffee, "We wait. Captain Dan has men searching everywhere."

"They don't know where to look for these black hoods," Tommy scoffed.

Dale turned and looked sternly at Tommy, "Then put your trust in Miles. He's escaped traps before. He'll get out of this one."

Tommy pulled out a chair at the kitchen table and plopped into it, "I guess that's all we can do."

In the darkness Miles Murdock could do nothing except wiggle and pry at the bindings on his wrists. Soon the skin was rubbed from his wrists. He gritted his teeth and continued. He had worked at his bonds for some time and felt they were loosening the smallest amount when he became aware of a stirring somewhere near him. Doc froze. He had thought he was alone. Listening he could hear scraping of cloth on the concrete floor and heard muffled groans that sounded like a gagged man.

Another prisoner changed things. Doc considered trying to make contact but realized two gagged men were not going to have much to say to each other. If they were left alone for any length of time they might attempt to untie each other but Doc had a feeling that someone would be coming to make a decision about the captives soon. Considering what had happened to the other captives so far, he thought their fate would be quickly determined. He decided to stay silent and play out his hand for the time being.

Sure enough, minutes later Murdock heard muffled voices nearby. They sounded like they were coming through a wall or door. Straining to listen he quickly decided the conversation was not in English? He could only catch a few words here and there, again it sounded like Spanish.

A key turned in a lock and a door scraped open. Footsteps entered the room. Doc remained motionless simulating unconsciousness. There came a harsh laugh and then the almost simultaneous sounds of something striking flesh and a deep painful groan. This was repeated twice more, followed by the sound of harsh laughter. Commands were given; Doc clearly recognized Spanish this time. As he heard the sounds of a body being moved, a foot prodded him sharply in the ribs. Doc gave out a low groan. There was a pause and then more Spanish. Footsteps retreated and Murdock was alone for the moment. He lay motionless worried that someone was observing him.

Soon footsteps returned and Doc was lifted by several hands. He was carried roughly from darkness out into fresher air. He could feel alternate bits of shade and sunshine through the burlap covering his face. He was carried for some distance. It grew darker and cooler and Doc decided he was being carried beneath leafy trees. The men carrying him were silent until minutes later one of them spoke, again in Spanish. Doc felt himself carried into a building. He heard the creak of a wooden floor and felt it beneath him as he was dropped rudely onto it. He landed hard on his right side. Pain jarred through his already sore arm. Stunned for a moment, Murdock vaguely heard a door slam and a key turn in another lock.

A few minutes of careful listening convinced Doc he was finally alone. He twisted around until he found a semi comfortable position and returned to pulling at the ropes binding his hands. He worked like this for several minutes until he realized he was feeling a sharp pain in his upper thigh. He wiggled around decided that something sharp was poking up through the floor. This was interesting.

Doc rolled and wiggled around until he could locate this object; first with his arm and then finally with his bound hands. It was a loose nail sticking up from the floor boards he rested on. The round head of the nail had been torn or bent and had a very sharp edge sticking upwards. "Yes!" Murdock thought to himself, "Finally a break." He began raking his wrist over the nail.

It took time but twenty minutes later the rope parted and Doc's hands were loose. Reaching up he peeled the sack off his head and looked around. He was in a rough wooden shed. The windowless building was approximately ten feet square and totally empty. Through rough cracks and knot holes Doc could see shaded light from outside. He quickly pulled his gag away and untied his feet. Doc stood up stiffly and attempted to stretch. He was stiff from being tied and he felt joints crack and tight muscles pull painfully as he worked circulation back into his limbs.

Surprisingly, Murdock still wore his wrist watch. It was nearly 3:30, almost three hours since he had been kidnapped. His suit jacket was gone and his dress shirt was torn and filthy. His tie was loose but still hanging from his neck. He removed it and stuffed it in a pocket. He had keys and change in his pockets but his wallet had been in his jacket. He padded quietly to the door and listened carefully but could hear no sounds nearby. The door was locked as expected. He did hear a bird call from somewhere close. He decided he was probably in the country somewhere.

Options were slim. Doc picked up the rough rope that had bound his legs and sat down next to the door. As he waited he wondered who the unlucky other captive had been. He hadn't got a good look at the man he had attempted to help in front of City Hall. Was it another prominent citizen? It was clear that whoever was behind the mayhem had come to town with an agenda. High profile attacks, kidnapping prominent citizens, destroying public landmarks; these events had to have a guiding hand. Could it be political? Was there foreign involvement? Certainly there were indications that foreigners were in town and involved in the chaos. When he got back to town he would have more work for Dale and Tommy.

Sometime later a branch cracked sharply outside the shed and footsteps approached the door. Murdock slid slowly to his feet and took the rope in both hands. A key turned in the lock and light flooded into the darkened shed. A hooded man stepped forward carrying something. Doc stepped forward and whipped the rope over the man's hood and jerked it tight on his throat. The man dropped something that hit the floor with the sound of broken crockery. He grabbed for his throat but Doc pulled tighter. As the man's hands flailed around, Doc lifted a knee into the man's back and jerked back hard on the rope. There was a reflexive jerk from the man and he gave off choking sounds. He clawed violently at his hood. Doc felt him sag and let go of one end of the rope. The man sagged to his knees still clawing at his hood. He managed to pull it off. It fell to the floor unnoticed as the man fell forward and rolled onto his side. Murdock stepped back. He knew instinctively that he had crushed the man's larynx. He could get no air and would be dead in seconds. Any pity he felt was quickly submerged thinking of how the hooded men treated their kidnap victims. The thought of Dale identifying his beaten corpse hardened Doc's heart as the hooded man's struggles grew weaker.

Murdock waited until the man's final struggles had ceased before quickly searching him. As the hooded man's feet drummed a final tattoo on the floor and he fell silent, Doc stepped forward. He quickly found a weighted leather sap in one pocket of the man's trousers. The man was not armed otherwise. He stepped around to see what his captor had dropped. The man had been carrying a pitcher of water. It had broken on impact and to Doc's frustration the water had spilled and run through the cracks in the floor. There was only an ounce or so pooled in one large shard. Doc gulped it down gratefully but it did little to moisten his dry mouth.

Before stepping out of the shed Doc took a hard look at his captor. He had very black hair and was of compact build. It was hard to tell with his features swollen and blackened but Doc felt sure he was dark complexioned as had been the gunman from the night before. Another foreigner? Shaking his head Doc stepped out of the building and looked around. He was in a small clearing surrounded by heavy forest. It was late afternoon and the sun couldn't be seen through the trees so he had no sense of direction. The air was warm and still; not a ghost of wind moved the surrounding tall trees. A narrow path led into the woods to his right. To his left across the small clearing a wider path disappeared though the trees. Which way had his captor come from?

Murdock was just about to flip a mental coin to decide which way to go, when a dark haired figure suddenly entered the clearing to his left. The man was not wearing a hood but he had one in his hand. Surprised he stared open mouthed at the disheveled physician. His decision made, Doc turned and fled down the path to his right. The path was narrow and nearly overgrown. He pushed through small branches growing across the path while brambles tore at his clothes. Doc could hear shouts somewhere behind him. The alarm had been raised and pursuit would soon follow he was certain. He pushed on as fast as he could. He only wished he knew where he was and where was running to.

His decision was quickly made harder. He came to a Y branch in the path. Doc skidded to a halt and tried to decide. Both paths seemed wider than one he was on so it made little difference. He ran to the left. The path was wider but not much. He caught occasional glimpses of the sun low in the sky and decided he was probably going roughly north or northwest. Not that that meant anything to the fugitive. Soon the path branched again. Actually it was crossed nearly perpendicularly by another path. Doc stopped and examined the crossing. Deciding that the crossing path was narrow and nearly overgrown Doc pushed on.

He soon came to another branch in the paths. Not wanting to loop back toward any pursuit Doc decided against left and instead took the right path. He had just started off again when he heard a gunshot echo through the woods. Doc picked up his pace. He decided the shot was probably from a handgun rather than a long gun but it sounded fairly close. His mouth was dry, his head was pounding and all he wanted to do was lie down and rest. Doc knew his pursuers were behind him though and from everything he had seen in the last few days they would not give up quickly and would certainly be ruthless if they caught up to him so he pushed on as fast as he could.

The pursuit went on. The forest paths turned and wound through the trees. They branched and bent back on themselves. If Doc Murdock had any idea where he was going that time was long past. He just kept moving as fast as he could. Several times he heard distant shouts and whenever he did he tried to move away from them. He considered leaving the paths and moving through the brush or even going to ground and attempting concealment in a patch of heavy undergrowth but he had no idea if his pursuers might be experienced trackers. Instead he pushed on and hoped for the best.

Then Doc's luck changed. The forest seemed to thin ahead of him. He quickened his pace and moments later he burst into a clearing. His hands on his knees, Doc rested for a moment attempting to get his breath back. When he stood up he was surprised. This was no small clearing. This was obviously a large field of cleared land. The grass was nearly waist high and small saplings protruded above the grass. The land was fallow now but had been cultivated in recent years if he was any judge. Doc set off at a trot across the field toward what looked like a row of trees three hundred yards away.

Doc had nearly reached the trees when he heard a gunshot behind him. He spun around. A man stood at the edge of the woods where Doc had come from. Grimly Doc spun and ran for the trees in front of him. Moments later he burst through the line of trees and stumbled waist deep into a creek that ran along the other side of the tree line. He waded across the stream into another overgrown field. Here he kept moving as fast as he could. The gunshot would gather the pursuit. His only hope was to find help; a farm house or major road where he could flag down a car, perhaps even a phone.

Murdock crested a small hill a quarter mile farther on and almost sobbed with relief; two hundred yards away stood a barn and farm house. Adrenalin now flowing strongly, Doc ran at his best pace forward. He could see the farm house clearly. There were two small outbuildings as well as the barn scattered about the tree shaded farm yard. Climbing a three rail fence he staggered toward the house.

As he limped closer Murdock realized something was wrong. The yard surrounding the house was overgrown. The barn doors were closed and nothing stirred in the yard. He stopped and looked around; the entire farm was silent; no clucking hens or barking dogs. The place had a deserted air about it. He trudged up to the back door, opened the tattered screen door and knocked loudly. No response. He knocked again and then stepped back. He then circled the one story building looking for signs of life but saw nothing. At the front steps he saw a ripped piece of paper fluttering on the front door. Doc knew what it was before he stepped up to examine it. Yes, it was a foreclosure notice posted by the sheriff.

Doc wiped his sweaty face as he considered breaking in. Then he stepped back and looked the house over. He shook his head as he realized there were no telephone wires entering the house just one lone power wire and he was sure that was disconnected. He turned away in disappointment. The good news was the long overgrown drive must lead to a road somewhere. He started that way when he heard a distant shout somewhere behind him in what sounded like Spanish. Pursuit close, Doc looked around and decided that the barn would give him the most immediate cover and perhaps a weapon.

Sprinting for the barn, Doc prayed that it wouldn't be padlocked. Luck was with him. The barn doors were closed only with a pivoting wooden bar. He quickly pivoted it up and pulled one of the doors open. Slipping inside he pulled the door closed behind him. Doc turned and almost immediately ran into the bumper of car he had not seen in the gloom. Cursing softly he bent forward and rubbed his shin as his eyes adjusted to the dark interior. The car was actually a small pickup truck. His hopes soared but Doc quickly tamped them down. The truck surely had not run in a long time.

Still, it was worth trying Murdock thought as he ran to the truck. He found the gas cap and twisted it off. Sniffing the nozzle gave off the strong odor of gasoline. He then grabbed hold of the bumper and heaved back and forth. A sloshing sound came from the open tank. Okay, he thought, "Maybe a gallon or so. Better than nothing." He pulled open the driver's door and felt around the dashboard. No key: First disappointment. Doc bit his lip for a moment then crept toward the barn door. He pushed one door open, leaned out carefully and looked around. The barn stood on a slight rise, the farm house off to its right and forward about twenty yards. The yard sloped gradually down past the farm house where it turned into an overgrown drive that sloped to a low wet spot about sixty yards away. It then gradually rose out of sight, probably toward some kind of road. Doc cocked his head and listened; nothing. He knew that shot had been to signal other searchers. They were no doubt closing in even now.

Doc hustled back to the truck and wiggled under the steering wheel and pulled down a handful of wires. Light was dim until Doc remembered his cigarette lighter. He didn't smoke but it had come in handy many times. Flicking it alight he examined the wires. He flicked it closed and pulled two wires loose. He bit down hard on each wire in turn until they parted. It didn't take long to then pull off some insulation on each and wind two ends tightly together.

Relighting the lighter Doc then picked out another wire. He repeated his procedure on this wire until he had it stripped bare for two inches. Taking a breath and sending up a silent prayer he touched the bare wire to the two newly crossed wires. The starter motor gave off a weak, "RRRrrrrrrrrrrr." Murdock sighed and tried again. Again a fading rrrrrrrrr sound tapered off to silence. The battery had sat too long. There wasn't enough charge to start the motor. Doc stood up and replaced the lighter in his pants pocket. Shaking his head he turned and searched around near the side of the barn and soon came up with a rusty pitchfork and an equally rusty shovel. He hefted them both and then making up his mind he dropped the pitchfork and slipped back to the door.

The shovel in his hands Doc looked out into the yard. He saw nothing at first but moments later a hooded man wearing work clothes came around the corner of the house, a pistol in hand. Doc ducked back inside the barn. A moment later he heard a shout. Peering through a crack in the barn door Doc saw the hooded man was now half way across the yard. Doc quickly stepped back and waited. A moment later he heard gravel crunch under a foot. He held his breath as footsteps grew closer. Finally a shadow fell across the barn door. Doc could see it through narrow cracks in the boards. Now!

Doc threw his shoulder against the loose hanging barn door. The big door flew open and caught the surprised man in the face. He flew backwards sprawling on his back. Doc ducked around the door and swung the shovel downwards once very hard. A quick glance around the yard and he picked up the hooded man's revolver and tucked it his waistband. He threw the shovel aside and grabbing the man's legs he dragged him quickly into the barn. A quick check of the man's pockets found half a dozen spare cartridges that Doc promptly requisitioned. He ducked down behind the front fender of the pickup and drew the revolver. At least he now was armed. He stared from the darkness of the barn out into the bright farm yard. Other searchers would be here soon. He glanced sideways at the truck. Perhaps he should hide inside the bed and take any searchers by surprise. His hand on the fender, Doc suddenly got an idea. His head snapped back around. He looked hard into the yard, his eyes measuring distances and angles. He rubbed his chin and thought, "It might just work."

Ducking around the open driver's door he quickly wrapped the loose wire around the two freshly crossed wires. He made sure the gearshift was in neutral, then he took a deep breath and with one hand on the inside door post and the other on the steering wheel he leaned forward and pushed. The little truck inched forward. Doc gritted his teeth and pushed harder. The truck rolled a bit faster. It soon rolled through the doorway into the light. The truck was moving slightly faster now and Doc pushed even harder. The ground sloped slightly downward and the truck rolled easier. It was still barely rolling forward at walking speed but every foot it traveled it was a little easier to push. Doc was sweating in the humid air but his adrenalin was flowing and he continued to push harder as the truck picked up speed. It was passing the side of the farm house and he was trotting now to keep pushing. From here the drive sloped downward to a low wet spot where a trickle of water crossed the gravel drive. Doc lunged forward grabbed the wheel and pulled himself into the cab. Behind the wheel he pushed in the clutch and shoved gearshift into high gear for compression. The truck was rolling now at perhaps five or six miles per hour. Doc knew he would get only one chance before the truck hit the incline on the other side of the low spot. He held his breath and let out the clutch.

The truck jerked as the little four cylinder engine fired, missed and fired again. The truck jerked a third time as the engine caught with a ragged roar. Doc pushed in the clutch and feathered the gas pedal. The engine was running rough and he could not let it die. Revving the engine he almost didn't hear the gunshot behind him but he certainly felt bits of glass sting his neck as a bullet hit the rear window. He didn't look around. Gunning the engine he let in the clutch carefully and the truck jerked forward. The truck splashed through the puddle at the bottom of the incline and Doc accelerated up the other side.

In the rear view mirror Murdock caught sight of movement as he felt the rear of the truck bounce on its leaf springs. A hooded figure was

"….Doc pushed even harder."

crouched on the rear bumper. As Doc watched, the figure threw itself over the tail gate into the bed. Doc floored the accelerator and the little truck bounced down the dirt drive throwing up a plume of dust behind it. The hooded man attempted to get to his feet but was being thrown around so badly by the rocking truck that he finally gave up and crawled forward until he was just behind the cab.

The drive had flattened out and Murdock could see fence lines and a mailbox at the head of the drive; there a road ran left and right. The accelerator still floored, Doc was trying to decide which way to turn when he became aware of movement next to him. The hooded man had thrown one leg over the side of the bed and got a footing on the running board. His left hand gripped the open window frame. This helped Doc's decision. As he reached the gravel road that fronted the abandoned farm he wrenched the steering wheel to the right. The little truck careened into a turn. Its right wheels came off the ground as it hit the mailbox, shattering the wooden post into splinters and sending the box flying up and over the roof. The hooded man yelled and threw himself wildly back into the truck bed.

Straightening the steering wheel dropped the truck back onto all four wheels. Speeding down the gravel road, Murdock began sawing the wheel back and forth. This had a severe effect on the man in back. Every time he tried to get to his feet he was thrown down again, ricocheting around the bed of the wildly swaying truck. Doc was aware of fences and fields flashing past. With one eye on the mirror watching the hooded man he almost missed the road bending sharply to the left. He braked hard and jerked the wheel over. The truck slid sideways in gravel almost running into the shallow ditch running alongside the fence line before it straightened up once more.

Unfortunately this had given the hooded man just enough time to swing over on to the running board. His shadow loomed up on Doc's left. Doc threw a wild elbow and hit the man in the ribs. He let out an unheard grunt and grabbed the side mirror with his left hand. Using this for support he threw a wild punch with his right that connected with Doc's cheek. Flinching Doc pulled the wheel to the right and then sawed it back to the left. The truck weaved wildly between the shoulders of the gravel road. The man clung to the side of the truck and threw another punch and another. Doc hunched down trying to take most of the blows on his shoulder. He still managed to catch a wild punch in the left eye that made him see stars. He threw another elbow into his attacker and continued swaying the truck back and forth.

Changing tactics his attacker reached through the window and grabbed Murdock's neck from the side. He gasped as the man's rough hand dug into his neck. The man then changed his hold and shoved Doc's head forward, painfully banging his forehead on the steering wheel. Stunned Doc lost control of the truck for a moment. The truck swung right and tilted that way as it scraped along a fence for ten yards before he wrenched it back into the middle of the gravel road. Grimacing through the pain in his neck Doc saw another sharp turn coming up; this time to the right. Instead of slowing he kept the accelerator all the way down. At the last second his attacker realized the danger and released Doc's neck to grasp for another hand hold. The truck roared into the turn. Doc held the wheel hard over and threw everything he had into another elbow jab. The elbow caught the hooded man just under his ribs. Already off balance and barely hanging on as the truck leaned far over to the left, he lost his grip and in an instant vanished behind the truck.

Miles Murdock straightened the wheel banging the two right hand wheels back onto the gravel surface and kept the pedal down. All he could see in the mirror was the plume of dust the little truck was throwing behind. Minutes later Doc slowed the truck. The road had once more come to an end with roads running left and right. Stopping the truck, Doc climbed out and stood on the running board. He rubbed his neck while he looked around. The fields he had been traveling past had been overgrown; probably from more than one abandoned farm. The depression, although now ending, had been hard on farmers in this part of the country. The field across from the truck at this point seemed well tended.

Murdock got back behind the wheel and turned left. He was sure he had come several miles from the abandoned farm but he still had no idea where he was. Keeping one eye on the fields to his right Doc sighted a large barn in the distance. He continued along and finally was rewarded with movement. Slowing along a long straight stretch of road he saw a man on a tractor far out in the field to his right.

Murdock pulled over and left the engine idling roughly. He didn't want to chance turning off the engine…he might not be able to get it started again. He honked the horn but it produced no sound. Grumbling Doc got out and stood in the back of the truck bed. Waving his arms over his head he tried to attract the farmer's attention. If he could get directions or better yet find the farmer's house maybe there would be a phone. A few minutes later the tractor finally stopped for a moment. When it started up again it turned and head Murdock's way. He blew out a long breath. It looked like his luck was finally turning. Doc turned and putting his hand on the truck's roof was about to vault over the side to the ground when he stopped. A plume of dust was coming down the road toward him.

Shading his eyes from the sun now low in the west Murdock squinted ahead. Moments later he identified a dark sedan coming down the road toward him. The hairs on his neck rose upwards. As the car rolled toward him Doc could soon make out several people in the car. Grumbling he ducked back into the truck and pulled the door closed. It looked like his hunters had found him. Gravel spurted from under the rear wheels as he pushed the accelerator down. The truck jumped forward. It closed on the sedan in seconds. Sure enough Doc could see hooded figures with in it as he aimed the truck straight for it. The sedan was moving faster as well. The vehicles closed with frightening speed. He was desperate and gritting his teeth he held the wheel straight. The other driver did as well. Then at the very last second the other driver swerved to the right and Doc rocketed past the car.

In his mirror Doc could make out through the dust the sedan turning around. He shook his head and floored the accelerator. The old truck responded as well as it could. The engine noise grew louder but his speed didn't increase that much. It didn't take long for the sedan to make up the distance. Soon its dark shape showed up in Doc's rear view mirror and quickly grew in size. The old truck was powered only by a small engine badly in need of a tune up. Soon the sedan was less than fifty yards behind coming fast. The two cars flashed across a gravel intersection. There was a sign at the crossroads but Doc couldn't get a look at it. The sedan roared up close behind him.

The oncoming car tried to pass but Doc Murdock swayed the truck in front of it. The car then tried to pass on the other side. Doc again blocked it. Finally the sedan dropped back a few yards. The two cars flashed past a farmhouse. Clean wash waved on a clothes line and a woman stood in the yard. A phone line paralleled this road and Doc longed to stop and ask for help but couldn't endanger innocent civilians. He kept his foot down and was taken unaware as the sedan closed and banged hard into his rear bumper. Doc's head was snapped back and he sawed the wheel back and forth to keep control.

The road bent to the left and then straightened. The sedan closed again and Doc expecting another ram was surprised when he felt sharp impacts and the windshield starred in front of him. They were shooting now. Great!! What else could go wrong? The road bent sharply to the right.

Doc held the wheel over to the right his wheels dangerously closer to the shallow ditch and screeched through the turn throwing gravel everywhere. His pursuers, in a better car, stayed right with him. Suddenly a new danger appeared in front of the fleeing truck.

Ahead Murdock could see a stop sign and a white striped barrier on the other side of a paved road running left to right in front of him. A major intersection loomed. As he watched Doc saw a car flash across his vision on the paved road ahead. If he stopped or even slowed his pursuers would have him. Doc gritted his teeth and held the pedal down. The intersection grew larger and he could see it was a wide major road. Trees lined it. Left or right?

Doc chose right. He waited until the last second and then tromped on the brake pedal as he cranked the steering wheel hard over, praying there was no approaching traffic. The tires screamed and the engine whined as the truck ran the stop sign and rounded the corner on two wheels. Centrifugal force pushed the car far out in the other lane but thankfully there was no oncoming traffic at that moment. The truck fell back onto four wheels as it straightened up. Close behind the sedan also ran the stop sign as it screeched out onto the paved road. It remained just yards behind. This paved road was in better shape but Doc could not use it properly. The little truck was running full out and the engine didn't sound good to his ear.

Ducking as more bullets thudded into the truck, Murdock didn't see the oncoming car swerve over to the side of the road in shock as the two vehicles flashed past it. The occupants stared open mouthed as they watched the beat up pickup truck flash past closely pursued by the sedan full of hooded men. The sedan accelerated and tried to pass again but Doc swerved to block it. The sun shining through trees onto his left cheek told him he was traveling north. He looked in vain for road signs but could read none even though they passed several side roads, all on the right. Then, suddenly Murdock knew where he was. This was River Road, somewhere North of Akelton. Beyond those trees to the left somewhere was the river.

A new danger was fast approaching. A bus was traveling north ahead of the two adversaries. Doc was closing fast on the slow moving vehicle. The road wasn't perfectly straight but he could see far enough ahead to pull into the oncoming lane. A quick glance to his right as he passed the bus showed surprised faces pressed to the windows as the truck, closely followed by the dark sedan, flew past. More gunfire crashed into the battered truck as they passed the slow moving bus.

Both vehicles pulled back into their own lane ahead of the bus just in time to dodge an oncoming auto zooming past in the opposite direction. Doc pulled the borrowed revolver from his belt and reaching behind him knocked enough glass loose to point the revolver out and fire. He didn't even try to aim. He was just trying to keep the hooded men at bay. They passed another car the amazed occupants gaping at the wild auto duel. Doc fired again but now he was becoming concerned with the truck. The engine had developed an ominous knock and steam was coming from under the hood. He had not had time to check the radiator.

The road vaguely followed the bends of the river while heading always north. Now the two vehicles were climbing slightly on a long grade. Murdock caught glimpses of the river reflecting the setting sun off its shimmering surface. The truck was laboring and on the upgrade the sedan made its move. Doc tried to block it by swerving into the oncoming lane. The sedan jerked back to the right and there was a metallic scrape as the sedan muscled alongside the truck. Doc pointed his revolver out the passenger window and fired his last shots just as the sedan swerved hard into the truck's right side. Tires smoked as he tried to keep his vehicle on the road but the bigger vehicle pushed the truck toward the opposite shoulder. Unable to hold the road Doc sideswiped bushes. Then with a clang the sedan gave one more powerful lurch into the truck's side. The little vehicle plunged off the road into heavy undergrowth.

Doc Murdock jumped hard on the brake pedal and whipped the steering wheel to one side, just missing a large tree. He tore through bushes and over small saplings. Finally the truck burst into the clear. The setting sun was ahead of him. Its last rays reflected off the river's surface. The truck flew off the low bluff in a graceful arc. For a moment the truck seemed to float through the air. Frozen in surprise, Doc could only squeeze the steering wheel in a death grip as the truck tipped forward and plowed into the river nose first. There was a tremendous splash. If anyone had been watching they would have seen the truck bob around nose down, the cab submerged for a few seconds before it slid under the water in an explosion of bubbles.

The sedan skidded to a stop a hundred yards down the road. The driver changed gears with a grinding noise and quickly reversed to the ragged opening in the bushes. A passing car saw four armed and hooded men jump from the car and push into the bushes. In moments they were standing on the edge of the bluff staring at the river. Below them a few lonely bubbles of air burst in the midst of an oily sheen on the river's surface. Bits of debris floated down stream with the current. There were loud comments in a foreign language and a few laughs as one man was roughly thumped on the back. Moments later, guns holstered the men were climbing back into their sedan. A curious car traveling north on River Road had stopped to see why the dark sedan had seemingly been abandoned in the road. At the sight of the hooded men it quickly fled. The sedan reversed in the road and headed south toward town.

+++

Dale paced nervously back and forth in her apartment. Tommy had left hours before to troll his underworld contacts for information on his missing Boss. The young nurse's features were twisted with fear. She knew how capable Miles was but she had a horrible sinking feeling when she thought of him captive of the hooded men terrorizing Akelton. Her stomach was a block of ice. The doorbell rang.

Dale threw herself at the door, hope filling her heart. She flung it open to find a solemn looking Dan Griffin standing on her threshold, hat in hand. Dale threw a hand to her mouth in fear, "Oh no!"

Dan spoke quietly, "May I come in, Dale?"

Wordlessly she stood aside as Griffin entered. With the door closed Dale leaned against it and whispered, "What is it?"

Griffin cleared his throat as his hands unconsciously crumpled his hat, "Well, uh nothing is certain but I thought you should know that…"

A tortured whisper tore from Dale's lips, "He's gone, isn't he?"

Griffin held his hands up in defense, "We don't know that, Dale. Miles is a survivor. These stories may just be . . ." He trailed off and tried not to catch Dale's eye.

"What stories?"

Griffin grimaced, "Well, late this afternoon we received reports of some kind of disturbance out on River Road, north of here on the road to Chesterfield. We've collected multiple reports of a sedan filled with hooded men pursuing a single man fleeing in a pickup truck. Apparently there was shooting. The two cars barely avoided hitting several autos and a bus." Griffin again fell silent.

Dale knew the answer but had to ask, "What happened?"

"Uh, apparently the sedan ran the pickup off the road. It uh …it uh, ran off the bluff into the river." He finished lamely.

"No!"

Griffin was confused, "No what?"

"No. That couldn't have been Miles. And if it was he's not dead."

Griffin chewed his lip for a moment before adding, "Uh, we have multiple descriptions of the truck's driver. He was a tall man with black hair wearing what looked like a white dress shirt." He held up his hands in self-defense before continuing, "I know it's not definite proof. But I thought you had to know in case, well in case . . ."

Dale straightened up and seemed to stand a little taller, "Miles is not dead. I'd feel it if he were. I don't know who that poor man in the truck was but I know that it'll take more than a few of these hooded killers to beat Miles." Dale was getting red faced with anger. She took a deep breath and asked, "What's being done?"

Griffin cleared his throat and tried to look upbeat, "We've got boats on the river now searching for the driver of the pickup. We'll drag the river for the wreck if we have to. I've sent patrols out on River Road looking for signs of these hooded men but . . ." Griffin grimaced again, "The Mayor has every available man guarding City Hall and other public buildings. We've called up reserves and asked the county Sheriff and State Patrol for more men but we're stretched pretty thin. Believe me, Dale; we'll do everything we can to find Miles."

Dale just nodded. After a few more reassuring words Griffin took his leave. In the hall he looked back at Dale, "For what it's worth, I don't really believe a few killers could get the best of him either. He'll be back." Dale managed a weak smile as she closed the door on the retreating figure of the detective. With the door closed she leaned against it for a moment and then slid to the floor her head in her hands.

CHAPTER TEN

Doctor Miles Murdock clung weakly to a broken chunk of timber floating down stream. His arms, shoulders and head were draped across the rough surface. He barely kicked his legs trying to save what little strength he had left. It was dark on the surface of the water. The river at this point had widened out as it entered the bay so the nearest lights were far across the nearly moonless, still water. It was too dark to read his watch and he wasn't even sure it still worked after being immersed in the river and of course the shock of the wreck.

The wreck! Doc thought back…he had been run off the bluff so quickly that all he had time to do was brace his hands on the steering wheel before the truck hit the water. The impact had banged his forehead hard on the steering wheel and stunned him for several moments. He came to his senses as the water closed over the cab and submerged him. Holding his breath he reached through the open window groping for the door handle. Thirty seconds later he gave this up and instead pulled himself through the open window. Swimming clear of the sinking vehicle Doc found himself upside down and momentarily disoriented. He finally got himself pointed in the right direction and swam strongly for the light.

His lungs burning, Murdock frantically stroked for the surface. Then he stopped. If he broke the surface below the bluff the hooded men would certainly be waiting with drawn guns to finish him off. Reluctantly he contorted his body around and began frog kicking hopefully in the direction of the current. Staying as far underwater as he could, he kept this up for what seemed like eternity. His lungs on fire and seeing bright spots behind his eyes Doc was finally forced to the surface. His head exploded out of the water and he whooped out a huge breath of carbon dioxide to suck in sweet air. Treading water he sputtered and spat water while he sucked in precious oxygen.

It took a moment to sink in before Doc realized there was no gunfire whistling past his head. Looking around he realized that he was near the east bank of the river, almost in the shade of the now lower bluff. He stroked closer to the shore until he was in its protective shadow. As he floated there Doc estimated from the shoreline that he was over a hundred yards south of the high bluff he had flown off of. Even now he was being swept further downstream by the current.

Murdock turned over and floated along on his back while he rested and got his breath back. It was quiet and almost pleasant floating along on the river's surface. The sun was so low in the sky that most of the river's surface was in shadow. The sun would be down in moments he judged. He considered swimming to shore and looking for a ride back to town but quickly discarded this thought. If the hooded men thought he was still alive they would be patrolling along River Road. He grimaced at the irony of the situation: The enemy patrolling the road instead of the police. How had things deteriorated so quickly in just a matter of days? Doc shook his head. He was no closer to finding the villain behind the Blackness than he had been Friday night. He lay back and let himself be swept along. What was the hurry? The river was sweeping him back to Akelton after all.

Darkness fell and the river darkened. Murdock was just thinking of swimming for the darkened shore when his head bumped painfully against something hard. Flipping over he grabbed hold of whatever it was expecting a log. Instead he found a four foot length of cut timber floating in the river. Gratefully he heaved himself half onto it and rested his head on the rough surface. Now at least he would arrive back in Akelton in style. Doc was very tired. He closed his eyes to rest.

Now hours later, holding onto the timber and kicking strongly Murdock neared a deserted wharf. He was in the upper reaches of Akelton's bay. The commercial piers were much farther along. This area he was in seemed to be occupied by small fishing boats and private craft. As he neared the small wharf he bid the friendly timber a fond good bye and swam toward a small rowboat tied to the worn pilings. Climbing out onto the wharf he scanned his surroundings as he dripped water. The only building in sight seemed to be a small darkened warehouse. Doc quickly untied the rowboat and hopped in. Unshipping the oars he rowed out into the current and headed down the bay.

Murdock regretted borrowing the boat but he needed it. After this was all over he vowed to find and reimburse the owner. He had come up with the rough outlines of a plan while he floated and he needed the boat to help him find a quiet place to re-enter Akelton inconspicuously. He pulled strongly against the oars.

An hour later Doc climbed onto a larger pier. He let the now empty row boat float away in the darkness. Doc flitted quietly through the darkness to conceal himself next to a darkened warehouse. He had chosen a quiet area of the mid bay to re-enter Akelton. It was after ten o' clock. Doc had been shocked to find his watch still ticking when he had checked it an hour before. Impressed, he decided it paid to buy quality goods. He slipped quietly off the dock and into a shabby industrial street. He quietly searched until he found what he was looking for; an unlocked window in the wall of a closed and abandoned warehouse across the street from the docks. Climbing inside he found a pile of discarded newspapers and cardboard, made a rough place to lie down and settled down in the darkness.

Murdock had considered finding a pay phone and calling Tommy or Dale for help but had reluctantly decided against it. In his present disreputable state anyone seeing him would probably call the police. Right now he needed to remain missing. He knew it was cruel to keep his friends in suspense over his safety but right now it was better if people thought he was dead. It would give both he and the Purple Scar more room to maneuver.

Doc settled back to think. He was physically exhausted. His head still ached from multiple abuses. His throat was sore and turning his head caused lightning bolts of pain to shoot through his neck. He was stiff and it hurt to breathe due to his tender ribs but he was not ready to sleep. There were plans to be made.

The man behind the chaos enveloping Akelton set the metallic cylinder down on his desk and walked across his luxurious study. The room was dimly lit only by a green shaded reading light on the desk. Reaching the French doors he threw them open and stepped out onto the tiny balcony. There was little light illuminating the grounds of his headquarters. Instead he looked up at the quarter moon rising in the east. He breathed deeply of the warm humid air. Things were going well…very well. Oh there had been the incident with that stupid man. It was embarrassing that he had escaped but Murphy had assured him the man was dead; drowned when he was forced off the cliff into the river. That was good. There had been plenty of witnesses to spread the word. The death of a prominent doctor would only spread the terror and chaos. Still the guard had been careless and though he had paid with his life, the rest of his men must be more careful.

The man smiled. With the capture of Russo he could now move on to other matters. His initial revenge was complete. Now for the next step; the chaos was increasing. The city was on the verge of panic. And best of all that masked fool the Purple Scar had barely put in an appearance. He had been wary of Akelton's protector because of stories told about the masked terror but so far his Blackness and his well-trained men were keeping the masked menace at bay. With no clues to his whereabouts and no connection to local criminals the Purple Scar had been frustrated in his sad attempts to interfere with the man's plans

Yes things were going well. A few more days and his plan would be complete. Soon Akelton would be ripe for the picking. The man looked up at the stars showing through thin wisps of cloud: perfect conditions. He smiled.

CHAPTER ELEVEN

Doctor Murdock woke up and was disoriented for a moment. He shivered slightly in the cool air. Pale light was coming from the window he had crawled through the night before. He judged it was not long before sunrise. Soon the heat of another day would warm him up. He sat up with a groan as his body reminded him of all that had happened in the last twenty four hours. He hurt all over. He stood carefully and attempted to gently stretch out his battered body. His right arm was still tender from the blow it had received Saturday but it seemed to be healing. His left eye was swollen half closed. His right cheek hurt as well and he could feel blood and matted hair where he had been hit over the head by a club. His head still hurt but it wasn't throbbing alarmingly as it had been. Doc decided he must have been concussed but he seemed to be recovering. He was bruised everywhere. But there were no stabbing pains when he breathed so none of his ribs were broken.

Removing his shoes and still damp socks, Doc wiped the dried mud and dirt from his now badly scuffed shoes. Replacing his socks and shoes he dusted off his trousers as best he could and left the warehouse. His once white shirt was now dirty and the pocket and one sleeve were ripped. He made a sorry sight as he walked through the warehouses toward the city center. Trying to help his appearance he rolled his sleeves up above his elbows. It looked strange on a filthy dress shirt but at least it concealed the ripped sleeve.

The docks were busy with ships and trucks being loaded and unloaded and roughly dressed workmen passing to and fro. He wasn't attracting much attention but that would change as he neared downtown. By eight o'clock, Murdock found himself in a run-down part of the city. Ironically he was only a half dozen blocks from his Down Street clinic. Even in this poorer section of town Doc was attracting a few odd looks. Deciding he needed better clothes, Doc considered the situation. His wallet was gone but he did have over two dollars in change in his pocket. He started looking around for a cheap second hand store.

Standing on a corner, Murdock saw a thin, shabbily dressed man loitering nearby. As a man in a suit passed him the thin man deliberately bumped into him. Doc watched interestedly as the thin man slid the other man's wallet out of his coat and into his own pocket. The two men apologized and parted ways. The pick pocket then walked away past Doc who fell in behind him.

Doc followed the thief for over a block before he made his move. Opposite a narrow alley he took two quick steps, grabbed the man by the back of the neck and jerked him sideways into the alley. Using this momentum he slammed the little man face first into a wall. The thief gasped in pain as his face and chest smacked the brick wall. Pressing on the thief's neck to immobilize his head, Doc whispered harshly in his ear, "Thought no one saw you lift that wallet eh? Well, I see everything."

"No! It's not what you . . ."

His words faded as Doc snaked the stolen wallet out of the thief's pocket. He leaned in and whispered, "I suppose you thought you were too small time for the Purples Scar to bother with, didn't you? Well, you were wrong."

"But, but, I uh . . ."

"Shut up! I'm in too much of a hurry this morning to beat the tar out of you and leave you for the cops so I'm gonna give you one chance. Either find an honest job or get out of town. If I catch you lifting another wallet, they'll find you floating in the bay. Understand?"

The terrified thief nodded, his face rubbing against the rough bricks. Keeping a firm grip on the thief's neck, Murdock pulled him away from the wall and forced him face down in the filthy alley. Leaning down he grated out, "Stay here until I'm gone. And remember what I said." He stood up and stepped quickly out of the alley. Out on the sidewalk he walked away and didn't look back.

A block away Doc took the wallet out and examined it. There was a total of nine dollars in it. He pocketed three dollars. After remembering the name and address of the wallet's owner he stepped to a nearby mailbox and slid the wallet in through the slot. It would be safe there. Doc had confidence that the next mailman to empty the box would turn the wallet in at his post office. It would eventually find its way home to it owner.

A half hour later Doc walked out of a second hand clothing store. A soft flat cap placed carefully on his head covered his black hair. A clean and not too worn light weight jacket now covered his dirty shirt. Now semi-presentable Doc walked toward the center of town. Ahead he heard a high pitched voice calling out loudly, "Read all about it. Prominent citizens kidnapped! Unknown Blackness terrorizes city!"

Reaching into his pocket Doc stepped up to the news boy, "Here boy. Keep the change." He handed the boy a dime and took a morning newspaper while acknowledging the boy's thanks. Newspaper in hand Doc crossed to a diner and took a seat at the counter. He ordered coffee and a donut and opened the paper. The lead story on page one would have troubled Doc more if he hadn't known the truth. It reported on the kidnapping of wealthy factory owner and business man Frank Russo and well known plastic surgeon Dr. Miles Murdock. The last half of the article consisted of a rather lurid recounting of the chase along River Road. At least a half dozen people identified the driver of the truck that ran into the river as Dr. Murdock. The article concluded with talk of the police investigating. So, it was Russo who had been attacked on the street Doc mused. He had known the man by reputation but not by sight.

The rest of the front page was filled with stories of the crime wave striking Akelton. On page two an article caught his eye; the body of Morris Bannerman had been found in a city park late last night. Doc shook his head and continued reading. Whoever was behind these kidnappings certainly did not leave his victims alive for very long. The rest of the news was all bad. In the last forty eight hours many banks and jewelry stores had been robbed by gangs of men. Some had worn hoods. Smash and grab raids had plagued many businesses around town. More city property had been vandalized overnight.

Frowning Doc turned to the editorial page. Sure enough there was a scathing editorial by Wells, the editor, accusing the Mayor and police of incompetence. It called on the Mayor to have the governor declare a state of martial law and send in troops. If he did not; it demanded he resign. A letter to the editor penned by Councilman Paley caught Doc's eye. It was not as strident but it certainly cast the Mayor in a bad light and called for 'new blood' to lead Akelton into the future. Doc grimaced. Paley was certainly making use of this crisis to boost his campaign. And Wells the editor seemed to be conspiring with him.

His donut and coffee reminded Murdock he hadn't eaten in nearly a day. As he munched he thought about the kidnappings. Macpherson had been on the council but the other councilmen and the Mayor had not been threatened …yet. So were the kidnappings political? Paley was certainly profiting from the bad publicity. But who else? Darlan and MacPherson had previous dealings with each other. Did Bannerman and Russo have a history with the first two kidnap victims? There were a lot of questions that needed answering.

Paying with some his precious pocket change Doc left the diner, walked two blocks and caught a street car going downtown. He got off opposite

"…caught a streetcar going downtown."

a large multi-story building. The sign on the building proclaimed it to be headquarters for the *Akelton Daily Times*. Doc entered the lobby and walked directly to the building directory. As he expected the newspaper records, more commonly referred to as the 'morgue' was located in the building's basement. His rather shabby appearance caught a few curious looks but once in the stairwell to the basement Doc met few people.

The morgue was run by a rather elderly man who seemed pleased to have visitors. When asked he told Doc he only kept working there because retirement was so lonely. To keep him happy Murdock gave the old codger a good story about trying to locate information on older relatives. The attendant showed Doc how the aisles of newspaper records were organized and hovered for a while trying to be helpful. Finally deciding that Doc wasn't very talkative, he wandered back to his desk.

It took a while, hours in fact before Doc Murdock felt he had a handle on the information he wanted. Darlan, MacPherson, Bannerman and Russo did know each other. It turned out that twenty years before they had been up and coming entrepreneurs. Newspaper stories repeatedly reported on their activities. Individually and together in various combinations the four had made great fortunes in Akelton's heady growth years. Many of their dealings were in real estate but also in acquisitions of new or established businesses.

The four of them had done very well during the enthusiastic business climate of the "Roaring Twenties" but more importantly they had all consolidated their investments and weathered the "Crash of '29" surprisingly well. By afternoon Doc felt he had a good grasp on the men's dealings. MacPherson had turned toward politics in the last few years. The others were now considered part of Akelton's elite in the social and business realms. Interestingly he could find no sign of crooked dealings or accusations of illegal activities among the four, either together or separately. Certainly they had been aggressive and even ruthless, but they seemed to have done nothing illegal. So why had those four men been singled out for kidnapping? Though Doc still didn't have all the answers he felt like he was finally getting a handle on a few things.

Doc was tempted to snoop around the *Times* building while he was here. Wells' hostility to the Mayor interested him. However his watch and his growling stomach told him it was after 3 pm and he decided to finally get in touch with Dale and Tommy. He caught a street car across town that took him within a few blocks of Dale's apartment building. He was walking down her street when he saw a dark Ford sedan pull up near Dale's building. Doc instantly recognized the familiar figure of Tommy Pedlar behind the wheel. Quickening his pace he reached the sedan, jerked open the passenger door and plopped himself onto the seat next to his startled aide just as Tommy opened his own door.

For a moment Tommy gaped open mouthed at the battered physician as Murdock smiled back. Then Tommy reached out and grabbed him with both hands, "Doc! It's you!"

"I'm afraid so, Tommy."

A smile lit up the little man's face, "I knew those hooded guys couldn't get the best of you!"

"Well, I can tell you it was a close thing there for a while but I made it home safe and uh, fairly sound."

Taking in Doc's rather battered form Tommy tried to frown but couldn't hold back his smile, "Geez, just wait'll Dale finds out."

"I'm on my way up to see her now. The three of us need to talk. But first I need you to fetch some things for me. I'm tired of running around naked out here. It's bad enough these guys have us out numbered but now I don't even have a gun."

"Just tell me what you need, Doc." Murdock gave his aide detailed orders before sending him on his way. Tommy waved as he drove away. Minutes later Doc stood before Dale's door. At the knock Dale hurried to the front door of her apartment. She was expecting Tommy with hopefully good news. Dale threw open the door and momentarily stared open mouthed at the battered figure standing in her doorway. She yelled, "Miles!" and threw herself into Doc's arms.

Sometime later Doc whispered in her ear, "Don't you think we should get in out of the hall?" Holding back tears Dale nodded. The two entered the apartment closing the door behind them. Dale led Doc to the sofa. As he sank down on the soft cushions he sighed. Dale still had hold of one of his hands, "We were so worried."

"I know darling. I'm sorry. I couldn't get word to you at first. Then last night I decided it might be better if I stayed dead to the public for a while. I worked my way slowly across town today and here I am. You and Tommy are the now the only ones who know that Dr. Murdock is alive and well."

Dale raised an eyebrow, "You haven't spoken to Dan yet?"

"No. I will soon. But I'll swear him to secrecy as well. For now it's better if everyone thinks that Miles Murdock is dead. It will give the Purple Scar room to work."

"You'd better talk to Dan soon. He's worried about you as well and he has news."

"Really?"

"Yes, he called here today to tell me about the search at the river. He also told me the hooded man who was shot behind City Hall was definitely foreign."

Doc was interested, "Did they identify him?"

"No. It was something about the coroner identifying his dental work as being definitely done outside the U.S."

"That is interesting. What else have you and Tommy found out?"

Dale gave Doc a stern look, "Oh, no you don't, mister. I want to know where you've been and what you've been up to. You look terrible. Were you really in that car that went over the cliff into the river?"

Doc leaned back with another sigh, "Tell you what, I'll trade the story for some aspirin and an ice pack."

Dale stood up and shook her head, "You're going to need more than that. You look like twelve miles of bad road. You talk and I'll see about getting you patched up."

While Dale fetched water and bandages Doc started his tale. It took a while but by the time she had cleaned and bandaged his scraped forehead, the nasty wound on the back of his head where he had been struck and painted his many scrapes and cuts with merthiolate, Murdock had finished his tale.

As she gathered up the first aid pieces she smiled weakly, "Well, I can't match that story but I have found out something that may be helpful."

Leaning back on the sofa and holding an ice pack to his eye Doc asked, "And that would be?"

"Well, I called old Mrs. Kreigle last night. She has been following the news and had heard about the kidnappings. She told me that the names Bannerman and Russo had rang a bell. I had been asking her about Darlan and Macpherson so those names were fresh in her memory. She told me she remembers some kind of scandal involving the four men a long time ago."

"Really? Did she have details?"

"Not really. She said it happened several years before the Crash; something about a suicide and scandal."

Doc looked thoughtful, "In those days the four of them were pretty big movers and shakers, I guess. From what I've read all four men did have dealings with one another but none of the information I've seen talked about any scandal or illegal activities."

"It might be worth looking into."

"It might be." Doc lay back on the sofa to think about this new development.

A half hour later there was a knock on the door. It was Tommy. He came in carrying a suitcase and a suit of clothes on a hanger, "I got everything you wanted, Doc." Murdock sat up and took the grip from Tommy, "Hang that suit in the bathroom, Tommy."

While Tommy carried out that order, Doc opened the case. Inside were a change of under clothes and all the gear he had asked for. Doc picked up a revolver, flipped out the cylinder, checked the load then closed the action. He had a mask in each hand when Tommy reappeared, "Okay Doc, I know you're in a hurry to get back out there, but I gotta know what happened."

Doc smiled and quickly repeated the account of his adventures. When he was finished he asked, "Dale's filled me in on her research. Have you heard anything new?"

Tommy looked thoughtful, "Things are nervous out on the streets. There's been a lot of talk that some of the local gangs are taking advantage of the chaos. I heard a couple of Malone's boys bragging about how anything they did was gonna be blamed on the black hoods. They just wished they had some of the Blackness to cover their escapes too."

Doc clenched his fist as he replied, "We'll settle up with Malone when this is all over. Anything else?"

"Well yeah, actually. I maybe got a line on these hooded guys."

Doc sat up straight, "What? What do you know?"

"Nothin' yet. But I'm going out to meet a guy later who might know somethin' about them."

"Good. I'm going too."

Dale who had been standing in the kitchen doorway spoke up, "Oh, no you're not. You're going to rest right here and get your strength back. Tommy can meet up with this man. He can call you when he knows more." She looked over at Tommy, "Is this man dangerous?"

Tommy shook his head, "Naw. He owns a little shop downtown. I just heard that he knows something about the hooded men. It shouldn't be dangerous."

"There you have it," she handed Murdock a fresh ice pack. She then gave Tommy a look, "Miles, needs to rest. We'll be here if you need us." Tommy stood up and clapped his hat on his head, "Right. I'll call later."

After Tommy had gone she brought out a blanket for Doc. He wanted nothing more than to lie back on the sofa and close his eyes but he had to do something first, "Dale, I want you to call Dan Griffin, say 'it's important.' When you get him on the line, give it to me."

Dale picked up the phone and started dialing. It took a few minutes but finally Griffin's gruff tones came across the line. Dale handed the phone to Murdock, "Dan. Listen carefully. Don't say my name. I was in that truck but I escaped and finally made it back but I need your help."

There was fast thinking silence before Griffin replied, "Alright, but what the heck is going on?"

Choosing his words carefully Doc said, "Right now the enemy thinks I'm dead. If I stay under cover I can continue to figure this thing out. I have a rough idea where the bad guys might be and I'm starting to get a handle on the abductions but I need time. If everybody thinks Miles Murdock is dead there will be more room for the Purple Scar to operate. Can I depend on you?"

There was a large sigh from Griffin, "Yes. I'm with you. But, are you alright?"

"I'm a little banged up but nothing a good night's sleep won't cure. Do you have anything new?"

Griffin scoffed, "Who has time to do any detecting. I'm spending all my time running around putting out fires. The Chief, the Mayor and anyone else with any influence has my detectives either guarding their fair skins or chasing off to the latest attack of Blackness. We're stretched awfully thin."

"I think that's what the enemy wants. He's keeping everyone off balance and busy chasing shadows. I'm getting closer to finding out what's behind all this but I still have work to do. What about this body at the morgue?"

"The coroner can't identify him past deciding he is definitely from overseas due to his dental work. He also appears to be of Latin American or perhaps a Mediterranean background from his looks."

"Well, that's a start. Stay safe, Dan. I'll be in touch as soon as I know more."

"Right. Take care." The two friends hung up simultaneously. Doc leaned back and closed his eyes. He spoke aloud to Dale, "That's taken care of; now about that nap." Leaning back on the sofa, Doc was asleep in seconds. Dale picked up the blanket and quietly covered his sleeping form.

CHAPTER TWELVE

Miles Murdock slept deeply. So deeply that he did not hear the phone ringing. He came awake when Dale touched his arm. She looked troubled, "It's Tommy. He's in trouble."

Doc was up in a flash. He grabbed the telephone in one hand and held the ear piece in the other, "Tommy? What's wrong?"

Tommy spoke in a whisper, "Doc, I'm in trouble. I was just gettin' the guy to spill when a bunch of them black hoods busted in and started shooting. I got him out the back but he caught a slug. He's hurt bad. We need you to pick us up."

"It's alright, Tommy. Just tell me where you're at."

"We're at Twelfth and Flower. I'm calling from a filling station. I can't stay here. We'll be in the alley behind Twelfth. Hurry, Doc."

"Hang on, Tommy. We're on our way."

Hanging up, Doc filled in the anxious Dale while he grabbed up clothes and ran for the bathroom. Minutes later he and Dale were in her car racing through the night.

Fifteen minutes after Tommy's call, Dale slowed her car a half block away from Twelfth on Flower Street. A darkened alley yawned across the sidewalk on the right. His pencil flash in one hand and revolver in the other, Murdock entered the alley. He felt a stirring in the darkness and Tommy's voice called out softly, "Is that you, Boss?"

Doc flicked on the light. Caught in its beam were two figures sprawled in the alley. Tommy held a man in his arms. It seemed like there was blood everywhere. Doc leaped forward. Kneeling he shone the light on the wounded man, "What happened?"

"We was going out the back door of his place when he was shot. The bullet went in his side. I've tried to keep pressure on it like you showed me, Doc. But he passed out a while back. Can you do anything?"

"We've got to get him someplace where I can work. Help me get him on his feet." Together the two men got the unconscious man on his feet and supporting him between them worked their way to Dale's car. She had a door open and they managed to get the man laid out in the back seat. Doc piled in after him while Tommy took the passenger seat. As Dale pulled out into the street she asked, "To the hospital?"

Tearing open the wounded man's shirt and examining the wound by flashlight Murdock replied, "No. He's in danger. The hooded men won't stop at shooting up a hospital if they really want to get him. Take us to Swank Street."

Dale turned right at the next corner and steered the car uptown, "That could be a problem. With you gone, both clinics are closed. Dan has officers watching both places in case the hooded men come around."

Doc leaning over his patient decided quickly, "Go around to the next block over. We'll take him in through the back alley entrance."

It was after ten o'clock and the streets were lightly traveled. As she drove Dale looked over at Tommy who was holding his arm and leaning against the door, "Tommy? Are you alright?"

The little man hesitated then whispered, "I'm afraid they got me too."

Doc's head came up, "What? How bad is it?"

"I caught one in the arm. It hurts like the devil but I don't think it's too bad."

"Damn! Dale we have to move quickly." But Dale had already pressed her foot down and her car shot forward. Quickly negotiating the darkened streets, she soon slid the car to a stop on a quiet street. Murdock was out first and carefully lifted the wounded man in his arms. Dale helped Tommy and the four people entered a narrow alley. This alley led to the concealed back entrance of Doc's Swank Street clinic.

A quick turn of a key and they were inside the clinic. Doc led the way to his operating room. Fortunately it was a windowless inner room. Before Dale led Tommy off to another examining room to look at his arm, Doc asked, "What's this man's name?"

His teeth gritted against the pain Tommy whispered, "Arturo Manero. He runs a flower shop on Tenth Street."

Murdock hefted the unconscious Manero onto the table in his operating room. Once there he cut away the man's shirt and positioned the bright lights over the table directly on the man's chest. He had a wound on his left side and a corresponding wound around on his back. Judging that the rear one was an entrance wound and the front an exit wound, Doc was relieved that he wouldn't be probing a for a spent bullet. He quickly moved to a cabinet and pulled on a white gown and mask. He was washing his hands when Dale returned, "How's Tommy?"

Dale too began washing her hands, "He's got a bullet wound in his right arm. The bullet exited cleanly and I think he's going to be alright but he's not going to be using that arm for a while. I stopped the bleeding. He'll hold for a while. How's Mr. Manero?"

Pulling on a pair of rubber gloves Doc replied, "Shot in the back, right side. He's breathing well so the bullet missed his lung. The blood isn't dark so it probably missed his liver as well. I think he's got some ribs broken but I won't know until we get in there."

Ready now, Doc Murdock began cleaning blood away from the wound while Dale prepared ether for their patient. Once the ether had been administered, Doc took a scalpel from Dale and asked, "Ready?"

Steady Dale replied, "Yes, Doctor." Murdock took a deep breath and leaned over the patient.

Later, as they moved Manero to a comfortable room quipped with a hospital bed Dale remarked, "That went well."

"Yes, he was lucky. The bullet missed all the important organs. It will take a while for that shattered rib to heal but I'm sure I got all the fragments out."

Proudly Dale smiled at her fiancé, "You would have made a wonderful surgeon, Miles."

Doc smiled modestly, "It's a good feeling saving a person's life but the work we do is important too, Dale. Let's take a look at Tommy."

Tommy looked pale and worn when they got to him. Dale had given him something for the pain so he could tell his story while Doc cleaned and bandaged his arm, "This guy Manero runs a flower shop on Tenth. It's right next door to one of the smash and grab raids them hooded guys did earlier this week. So he rushes out into the street and sees some of them getting away. He hears them talking and recognizes it because he speaks Spanish."

Doc nodded as he worked, "When I was held captive I recognized several of the men as speaking Spanish as well. I wish my Spanish was better I barely caught a few words. Did Manero hear anything important?"

"Just them talking about getting the loot back to their hideout. Not where it was though."

"Too bad we could have used a break like that."

"Didn't you get an idea where they took you, Boss?"

Murdock shrugged, "Its north of town. I have a rough idea where but I got turned around so much while escaping it won't be easy to find. So what makes Manero so important?"

"That's the thing, Boss. He doesn't know where they were going but he knows where they're from."

Doc raised an eyebrow, "How do you know that?"

"He told me."

"So what did he know, Tommy?"

"Manero told me the hooded men, at least the bunch he saw, were from Cuba."

"Cuba? How did he know that?"

"It's where he came from. He heard them talking and he claims the ones he heard sounded like they were all from Cuba. Accent or somethin, I guess."

"Where did you hear about Manero?"

"Talk on the street. I guess he told some of his friends and word got around. The bad guys must have heard too. They showed up just as I was talking to him."

Murdock thought this over as he helped Tommy down the hall to room equipped with a cot that Doc himself used occasionally. Why would someone go to the trouble of importing gunmen from a specific nation? Unless…that person had a connection to that part of the world. It was something to think about.

With their patients finally resting easily, Doc and Dale sat down together. What do we do now, Miles?"

"You are going home to get some rest. I'll stay here and keep an eye on our patients tonight. When you come back tomorrow morning, we'll get started again."

"Do you have a plan?"

Doc rubbed his chin, "I'd like to use your car and go looking for the place I was held but that's a long shot. Right now, I want to research this scandal the four victims were involved in. The newspaper and the library are the place to start. Things just aren't adding up. If some kind of revenge against Darlan and company is the motive for all this; why the foreign involvement? Importing gunmen from Cuba doesn't make a lot of sense. And why the crusade against the City?"

Dale nodded, "You won't have to use my car. That black Ford Tommy was driving is the car he bought for you. I'll bring it back here tomorrow morning."

"Good. It looked inconspicuous. Now you better get home. It's late. And be careful on the streets." Dale reassured Doc she would and after a quick kiss was on her way. After she left, Murdock carefully checked all the doors and windows and settled down to wait.

CHAPTER THIRTEEN

Dale returned to Swank Street the next morning via the concealed back entrance. Both patients had rested during the night and their prognosis looked good. Over coffee, Doc and Dale made plans, "I took a bus over to Twelfth and then drove the new Ford here. It's parked the next block over. Here are the keys. My car's here if I need it. Oh, and I brought some lunch fixings for our patients." Dale held up a large sack.

Doc smiled, "Good. Both our patients are resting easily. I'll try to check in with you in a couple of hours from downtown." Quickly donning a new mask he had made up the night before, the Purple Scar made his way out the back and through the alley to the street beyond. The Ford sedan that Tommy had bought was an inexpensive model several years old. It was quite inconspicuous but the engine fired up instantly and sounded strong as it settled down to idle.

The Scar drove carefully downtown. As he did, he noted signs of the terror gripping Akelton. More than a few shops were closed, traffic both foot and auto was lighter than usual. And there was a large police presence on the streets. The Scar noted that the block in front of City Hall was completely closed with barricades. Police headquarters was the same way.

Parking near the *Times* building the disguised Scar made his way into the building and down to the Morgue room. The same lonely attendant was working today. He seemed glad to have the company of the well-dressed man with the pleasant face. Unfortunately he was disappointed. This man did not want to make small talk any more than the shabbily dressed fellow yesterday had. This man also seemed intent on his mission just as his visitor yesterday had been. He showed the disguised Purple Scar to the section he was looking for and left him in peace.

The Scar knew what he was looking for but he didn't have exact dates. Thus he was forced to leaf through page after page of yellowed newspapers to find what he wanted. He finally located a headline reading "Noted financier found dead." The article talked about the apparent suicide of one Albert Sykes noted Akelton business man. The article inferred that Sykes had committed suicide due to recent financial set-backs. He had apparently suffered serious business losses near the time of his death. Even more interesting was the byline on the article. It had been written by Thomas Wells.

The Scar knew that Wells was a long time employee of the *Times* who had started out as a reporter many years ago. It seemed an interesting coincidence that he had written about the Sykes scandal and suicide.

As the Scar flipped back further for more information he realized that the Sykes in the article was the same man who had built the now restored mansion the Scar had visited. In clippings dated in the weeks previous to Sykes' suicide the Purple Scar discovered that Sykes had had severe business reverses. He had been forced to close several of his businesses and was on the verge of bankruptcy. And sure enough, Darlan, Macpherson, Bannerman and Russo's names came up repeatedly as business associates of Sykes. It would probably take a lot of deep research to figure out all the associations but the articles spoke of Sykes' loans being called and his businesses being acquired by ex-partners. The disguised physician did not doubt for a second that the ex-partners who had benefitted from Sykes misfortune had been the four kidnap victims. He was also sure that this was the scandal that Mrs. Kriegle had spoken to Dale about. Of further interest; many of the articles were written by Wells.

There it was; a concrete reason for someone taking revenge on the four prominent citizens. It looked like the four had most certainly been involved in the collapse of Sykes' business empire. The details didn't matter. Was someone from the past taking revenge for Sykes' disgrace and suicide? Who could it be? The Scar continued digging through background stories and finally came upon a mention of Sykes' personal life. It referred to his deceased wife and his young son. More searching finally found a reference to the orphaned boy being sent to live with distant relatives in Missouri.

His mind running over the possibilities, the Scar left the morgue after thanking the lonely clerk. Wells had covered the Sykes scandal as a reporter. He must surely have made the connection to the four kidnap victims. If he had this information why wasn't it in his paper's articles? It was certainly pertinent news. Was he concealing it for a reason? And why was he such a vicious critic of the Mayor? It looked as if Wells might be due for a visit from the Purple Scar.

As the Scar crossed the newspaper's lobby he stopped and bought a paper. The lead article concerned the finding that morning of Russo's beaten body dumped in a city park. He only skimmed the stories of more mayhem and chaos around town. They would tell him no more than he already knew. The police were on the defensive. He doubted that any of Griffin's detectives would have time to find out what was behind the wave of crime and terror. It was up to him to get at the truth.

Hopping back in his car, the Scar drove uptown to the Western Union office. There he wrote and paid for a telegram to be sent. It was addressed to Grant Stevens in St. Louis, Missouri. Satisfied, the Scar head back to Swank Street.

At his clinic he was pleased to find Tommy up and moving carefully around. The little man was cheerful and upbeat, "I'm fine, Doc." He moved his arm in its sling carefully, "I'll be back in action in a day or two."

"You just rest, Tommy. A slug through the arm is nothing to ignore." He turned to Dale, "And how is our other patient?"

"Mr. Manero came awake enough to drink some water and went back to sleep. There is no fever and I think he'll be fine in a few days. I'll try to feed him some broth when he wakes up next time. Did you find out anything this morning, Miles?"

"I sure did." Murdock quickly filled his friends in on his findings at the newspaper. He finished with his sending of the telegram.

Tommy listening keenly spoke up, "Stevens? Isn't that the Private Eye we used last year?"

"Yes. He was pretty good. I hope he can get a line on what happened to Sykes' young son."

Dale frowned, "You think the boy has returned for revenge on the men who ruined his father?"

"It's the only thing that connects all four of our victims. What I don't understand is all the other mayhem. If the Blackness and all this violence is just a cover for revenge it seems like overkill."

Dale mulled this over for a moment, "How old would the Sykes boy be now?"

Doc thought back to the article, "If it all happened over fifteen years ago then he would be about thirty years old or so."

"About your age. So where's he been all these years? He couldn't have been planning revenge for all that time."

"Maybe he has. If the now grown Sykes boy has returned he has a lot of help. Where would he get this Blackness and where did all these foreign gunmen come from?"

Dale looked thoughtful, "He must be a stranger in town then; a new face."

Doc rubbed his chin thoughtfully, "Someone like Councilman Paley. He moved here only a few years ago."

"He's about your age too, Doc."

Murdock nodded but added, "If it is Sykes behind this, there's a chance he's in league with someone in town. That would explain how he seems to know so much about Akelton."

"So do we just wait for an answer to your telegram? Isn't there anything else we can do?'

"Yes Dale, there is. You can go out this afternoon and check up on the honorable Alan Paley. Find out exactly when he came to town and where he came from if you can. He just moved up on our suspects list."

"Alright, and what are you going to be doing this afternoon?"

Doc smiled, "Taking a well-deserved nap." He rubbed his still swollen cheek, "I'm still recovering you know. Besides, the Purple Scar needs his rest; he might just be up late tonight."

CHAPTER FOURTEEN

That night just after nine o'clock, Doc sat next to Dale in the Ford. They were parked facing away, down the street from Thomas Wells' house, Dale behind the wheel.

When Dale had returned to Swank Street that evening Doc, Tommy and she had sat down to compare notes. Dale had told of her findings, "Paley came to town just over three years ago, supposedly from the Mid-Atlantic states. He ran for election for an open seat on the City Council two years ago. No one knows a lot about him except that he's a bit of a ladies man and everyone says he's smart. I did some research on him and sent a telegram to his university trying to find out if he actually is who he says he is."

Doc nodded, "Good work. I've been thinking of any other well-known people who are new in town but the only one I can think of is Dr. Sanderson."

Dale looked surprised, "The head of the Historical Society? I know he is relatively new in town but isn't he far too old to be the Sykes boy?"

"Yes, but that doesn't mean he's not working with someone else. And I find it an interesting coincidence that the new museum is in the old Sykes mansion." Then Murdock had told them of his plan to confront Wells and put pressure on the editor, "I want to know why he hasn't made the connection to the old Sykes scandal. Or maybe he has and is concealing it. Either way it's time to brace him and see what he knows."

After that, Doc prepared himself for his foray. He was surprised when Dale had insisted she would accompany him, "You need someone to look after you and with Tommy out of action I'm going and you can't stop me."

"But what about Tommy and Mr. Manero?"

Tommy had sided with Dale. "I can keep an eye on things, Doc. I'm feeling better by the hour."

Doc wasn't crazy about taking his fiancé into danger but he gave in gracefully; while thinking that he would have to have a word with Tommy about being overly helpful when this mess was all over. Now sitting beside her Doc pulled on his fearsome purple mask. He patted his pockets to make sure his various gear was in all place and looked at his fiancé, "You have your pistol?"

Dale pulled her .32 automatic out of her purse and nodded. The Scar continued, "Keep it handy. Stay here. I should be back in a few minutes. If you see anything unusual, sound the horn and then drive away quickly."

"But, I can't leave . . ."

"You can and you will. I'll be alright. You just get back to the clinic. I'll join you there later." Dale reluctantly nodded. The Scar opened the car door and quickly faded into the shadows along the residential street.

Wells house was a good sized two story affair set back from the street about thirty feet. From the deep shade under a large oak tree next door, The Scar studied the house. The drapes were closed but there was light on in what was probably a parlor or living room at the front of the house. A light burned on the covered front porch. A single light also burned in a second floor window along the side of the house. All seemed quiet. The tree lined street was only illuminated by street lights set wide apart.

The Purple Scar drifted quietly around the side of the building to the rear. The back yard was dark although the back door was brightly lit by another light over it. Deciding the doors were a little too brightly lit for his taste the Scar back tracked to the side of the house. The night was warm and humid. As he hoped many windows in the house were open to pick up any slight breeze that might spring up to move the heavy air around.

Boosting himself up, the Scar climbed through an open window into a dark room. Standing up he listened for a moment. He could hear distant voices and then what sounded like laughter. He chanced a quick one second flash of light from his pocket flash. He was standing in what appeared to be a sitting room. There was an upright piano, several chairs and small tables. The single door was closed.

At the door the Scar eased it open a crack. The voices were slightly louder. They were coming from the front of the house and to his ear they sounded like a radio program. He heard no other sounds. Stepping into the darkened hall the Scar crept forward toward an open doorway where light streamed into the hall. As he listened applause sounded and then

"You have your pistol?"

a musical theme. The Scar risked a quick look. In what appeared to be a comfortable parlor a middle aged woman sat with an open magazine on her lap listening to the radio. With a commercial now playing the woman picked up the magazine and continued reading. The Scar took this opportunity to ghost across the doorway and toward the stairs.

Once on the stairs, the Purple Scar kept close to the wall to avoid squeaky treads. He quickly reached the second floor. The hallway was dark; the only light came from a half open doorway. The sound of clicking keys came to the Scar's ears. Nodding he drew his revolver and strode quietly to the doorway and pushed it all the way open. Inside a man he recognized as Wells sat at a desk pounding away at a typewriter. The room was obviously a study. The editor was alone.

The Scar stepped into the room and whispered harshly, "Writing your next poison pen editorial?"

Wells started and dropped the lit cigarette that he had just picked up from the ashtray. His mouth dropped open as he started to yell but the Scar shook his head, "No noise." He then strode forward until he stood on the other side of the desk from the shocked editor. Finally Wells found his tongue and spoke in a hoarse voice, "What do you want here, Scar?"

"First you better put that cigarette out."

Wells swore and patted furiously at his dropped cigarette that was smoldering on some papers spread across the desk's surface. He held up a scorched sheet and glared at the masked man in his study, "You have no right busting in here. I don't care what they say about you, you're not much better than the men you kill."

The Purple Scar took this criticism silently. He then lifted his pistol and rasped, "Afraid you're going on that list?"

Wells went pale and held up a hand, "I'm not one of your criminals. I'm a legitimate journalist. I just report the news."

"That's what I want to talk about; the news. You've been writing some pretty nasty things about the Mayor. Why are you being so critical?"

Wells seemed surprised for a moment before answering, "It's the Mayor's responsibility to keep the city safe. He is obviously helpless against these hooded men. I'm just doing my job."

"And of course adding fuel to a good story sells newspapers doesn't it?"

Wells had enough honesty to at least look slightly embarrassed at the last statement, "There's no law against editorials."

"No, but there might be some against withholding evidence in a series of kidnappings," grated out the masked avenger.

Wells seemed surprised, "What are you talking about?"

"I've been trying to find out what Darlan, Macpherson, Bannerman and Russo have in common and now I learn that you've known all along."

Wells frowned, "I have no idea what you're talking about?"

The Scar leaned forward slightly as he hissed, "I'm talking about a young reporter writing stories about the financial dealings that bankrupted Albert Sykes and eventually caused his suicide. You knew all about those four and how they benefitted from Sykes' ruin and you said nothing to anyone. Why is that, Mr. Wells?"

Wells' mouth dropped open for a moment. When he finally found his tongue he spoke carefully and held up his hands, "Look, that was a long time ago. I had almost forgotten about it. Why it never occurred to me that that was why . . ."

The Scar cut him off with harsh whisper, "Not a very good memory for a reporter; maybe it's better than you're letting on. Maybe you do know who has come looking for revenge against those four. Maybe you're working with him; perhaps by writing some helpful editorials to stir up anger and sow confusion?"

Wells honestly looked surprised at this, "No that's not the way it is. Look Scar, I don't know who's behind all this chaos either. I may have been a little bit hard on the Mayor but it's not person---"

The Purple Scar's attention was suddenly caught by a car horn sounding from somewhere outside. The sound came clearly through the open window. The Scar cut off Wells with a sharp gesture. He turned toward the doorway just as there was a crash from downstairs followed immediately by a scream. He dashed into the hall and to the top of the stairs. The front door hung open and the hall was full of hooded men.

Backpedaling the Scar threw a shot down the stairs to delay his foes and ran back into the study. Wells had run around the desk. He tried to push past the masked man but the Scar grabbed his arm, "The hooded men are downstairs!"

Wells yelled, "My wife!" and pulled at the gloved hand on his arm.

"Don't be a fool they've come for you. We have to go!"

Keeping a firm hand on the editor's arm, the Scar pulled him out into the hall. A glance toward the stairs showed a frightening sight; Blackness was boiling up the stairs toward the second floor. The Scar caught a hint of movement but held his fire. It might be Wells' wife. This idea was swiftly abused by a shot whistling out of the Blackness in their direction. The Scar ducked and fired back once. Wells threw himself to the floor and covered his head as more shots arrowed out of the Blackness; striking the walls and whistling over the Scar's head. He fired four more times into the Black fog advancing down the hall and then his revolver clicked on an empty chamber.

Wells' prone form had already been swallowed up by the Blackness. Deciding he would be a fool to rush forward into the Blackness filled with his enemies, the Purple Scar reluctantly retreated down the hallway toward the rear of the house, thumbing fresh rounds into his weapon as he backpedaled. He heard a scream from somewhere unseen followed by yells and commands in Spanish. Reaching an open door the Scar ducked inside and slammed the door shut. It was hard to tell in the shadows but it appeared he was in a bedroom. He holstered his gun and moved toward the open window. The window looked out over the back yard.

Time was pressing so the masked avenger quickly threw his leg over the sill and dropped to the top of the back porch. He balanced there for a moment before crouching down and swinging his body over to hang from the edge. Dropping to the ground the Scar drew his revolver and cat footed around the corner of the house. A cloud of Blackness enveloped the front three quarters of it. He swung wide into the neighboring yard to get clear of the black wall. When he could see past the cloud to the street he saw an auto and a covered truck parked at the curb. Hooded men were bundling a form into the sedan while others piled into the truck. Gritting his teeth the Scar holstered his gun and sprinted forward. The car pulled away from the curb. The truck followed. He sprinted faster his arms pumping back and forth. The truck was starting to move past him as it gathered speed. His heart pumping as he reached the sidewalk, the Purple Scar threw himself at the side of the truck.

Dale waited quietly in the car, invisible in the darkness. She frequently turned her head searching for movement but the street was quiet. She couldn't read her watch in the darkness but she estimated that only ten minutes had passed since the Purple Scar had left the car when lights in the rear view mirror caught her eye. She watched as the lights formed into two sets of headlights coming from behind. As she watched, the headlights suddenly went out. Dale sank down peering over the back of the seat, her automatic clutched in her hand.

Seconds later a car pulled to a stop at the curb in front of Wells' house, a covered truck quietly pulled in behind it. As she watched hooded men spilled silently out of both vehicles. Without any verbal commands one of the men held his ground while the others swarmed toward the house. Her eyes never leaving the scene fifty yards behind her, Dale shoved her free hand down hard on the steering wheel. The horn immediately sounded long and clear.

Most of the hooded men crashed through the front door just after the horn sounded. As she watched the man who had been left behind turned her way drawn by the sound of the horn. Dale raised her pistol but instead of running her way, the man turned back toward the house and vomited a cloud of Blackness. Dale was thunderstruck. As she watched, the cloud spilled outward toward the house widening and climbing as it quickly enveloped the front of the house. Her amazement passing Dale focused and realized the Blackness seemed to be projecting outward from the man's hands. More importantly Dale saw that the man seemed to be wearing some kind of back pack she had not noticed before in the dim light on the street.

Unsure exactly how to help her man, Dale slid across the seat and threw open the passenger door. She stood up and aimed her pistol at the man seemingly directing the Blackness but quickly lowered it. What would happen if she shot him? He seemed to be controlling it but if he was hit what then? No one had figured out exactly what the Blackness was. Her decision was quickly made for her. The man turned and walked toward the sedan seemingly disconnecting himself from the cloud of Blackness that enveloped most of the Wells house. Seconds later hooded men spilled out of the Blackness onto the sidewalk. Two of them dragged a limp captive between them toward the sedan's open door. The rest began climbing into the truck.

Dale raised her gun up and was about to open fire on the sedan hoping to disable it when out of the corner of her eye she caught sight of a figure sprinting across the grass toward the vehicles. Grinning she dove back into the Ford, slid behind the wheel and reached for the starter. As she pressed it, the sedan accelerated past her filled with hooded men. Seconds later the truck followed, a man clinging to its side his feet scraping along the ground.

Dale shoved the car into gear and let in the clutch. The Ford lurched in pursuit, the passenger door swinging wildly before slamming shut. At the corner the sedan screeched into a right turn; the truck right behind. As she watched, the man clinging to the side of the truck gained a foothold and lurched upwards. Dale let out a sigh as he climbed upwards toward the top of the canvas covered stake bed truck.

Leaping as high as he could, the Purple Scar hit the wooden slats of the truck. His gloved fingers groped for hand holds and found some as his shoes dragged along the street. He clung there for a moment as the truck gathered speed. As it screeched into a right hand turn he was forced against the side. This gave him the time to finally find a foothold with the toe of one shoe. As he hung there movement at the corner of his eye caught his attention. He glanced to the left and saw the black Ford. Dale had fallen in behind the hooded men's parade and was following without lights.

For a moment the Scar was both elated and furious. Furious because the hooded men would not hesitate to run Dale off the road and capture or kill her if they discovered her presence. He was also elated knowing possible retreat was near at hand. He wanted to wave her further back but instead he trusted to Dale's good sense to protect her. Now he must find a way to stay aboard the swaying vehicle. Here was his chance to be led to the man behind all this chaos.

The Scar heaved himself upward until both feet were perched on the wooden slat sides of the truck. He decided his best bet was to stretch himself across the canvas covered top of the truck. He would use the metal support struts to support his weight. It would be uncomfortable but endurable. Stretching his upper body forward he leaned across the canvas and supported the weight of his upper body with his hands resting on two metal struts. Lifting one leg carefully upwards he raised it to the top of the canvas covering. At that point the truck followed the sedan into a left turn. His leg was swept back off the canvas to wave wildly outward. The truck straightened out and the Scar regained his balance. For a second time he swung his leg up the canvas side and got it over the top. The two vehicles speed increased as they reached a long straight street headed north. Carefully the Scar rolled over onto the canvas top. His weight totally supported by metal struts that cut into him at shins, thighs, stomach and chest. Finally lying flat to distribute his weight, the Purple Scar tried to relax.

Picking up speed the little convoy continued north. At the next corner the sedan made a sharp left turn. The truck followed. Stretched flat the Scar slid toward the right side of the truck. As his legs slid out over empty air he made a wild grab and his hand tore through the top of the canvas. Simultaneously his legs swung back toward the truck as it straightened up once more and both legs went straight through into the truck as the canvas parted with a ripping sound audible over the passing wind. The Scar let go with a curse and jack knifed into the darkened interior of the truck bed reaching for his revolver as he went. He smacked chest to chest into figure that was swaying back and forth to maintain balance. Blam! He fired point blank into the man's chest as they both went down in a heap.

There were two other hooded men in the truck. They had removed their hoods and were chatting among themselves when the masked vigilante suddenly fell thorough the canvas covering. As their third companion collapsed to the truck's bed holding his chest, the two gaped open mouthed in surprise for a split second before throwing themselves toward the two figures on the truck bed. One grasped a club in his hand.

The Scar retained his grip on his revolver as he rolled off the dead man. He raised it as man loomed toward him in the darkened interior of the truck. At that moment a club descended on his forearm. Screaming pain shot through his already tender right arm. The gun discharged as it was knocked from his numbed hand. On his knees, the Scar lunged forward taking the man in front of him in the stomach with his shoulder and throwing him onto his back. The Scar rolled off him to meet the man with the club. He deflected a wild swing with his left arm and punched back weakly with his still numb right. This blow barely threw the man off balance. Thankfully the rocking truck hit a bump at that moment that threw the man with the club against the wooden slats at the side of the bed. The Scar sensing movement ducked his head and turned. The first man's punch missed The Scar's head but knocked his fedora off into the darkness.

The Purple Scar replied with two quick left jabs to this man's face that drove him back. Feeling coming back in his right arm, he stepped in and swung a right cross to the man's jaw. The impact sent pain again shooting up his arm but man was driven back, tripped over the dead man and slammed to the truck bed on his back. A curse in Spanish alerted the Scar just in time for him to sway to one side as the man with the club again threw himself forward. The descending club missed the Scar's skull but clipped the side of his head and impacted solidly on his right shoulder. The Scar saw a burst of stars and collapsed to the truck bed stunned.

Standing over the downed avenger cursing in Spanish, his assailant was quickly joined by his companion rubbing his jaw. More yells in Spanish came from the truck cab. The man with the club crouched over the fallen crime-fighter for a closer look. At that moment auto headlights from a car following behind the truck flashed on illuminating the shadowy truck bed. Taken by surprise at the fallen man's horrible visage, the black haired man yelled out in surprise, "El Cicatriz Purpeo!"

Stunned for a moment, the Purple Scar lay on the truck bed and let his eyes come into focus. He could hear the foreign shouts around him. Then everything in the truck was thrown into stark relief as Dale turned the Ford's headlights on. This was just the distraction the Scar needed. He jerked his legs up to his chest then pistoned them straight out. Caught in the stomach one of his attackers grunted and was thrown back three steps. The back of his thighs caught the wooden slats at the side of the truck and he pitched through the flapping canvas of the hole made by the Scar's entry. His scream was quickly silenced.

Arching upwards, the Scar swung a left hook across his body at the other man crouched over him and caught him in the face. He fell backward. Rolling the other way the Scar scrambled to his feet in time to meet this last man's rush. The two stood in the back of the swaying truck trading punches. The Scar blocked a right punch and answered with one of his own that was only partially blocked. He blocked a left punch, grimacing as bolts of pain lanced up his arm and in answer he dropped his left shoulder and punched the man hard up under his ribs. His opponent's breath left him with a grunt. The Scar stepped in and then hit him with a short left hook, then quickly back handed him with the same fist. Finally he took another step forward and ignoring the pain he knew it would cost, caught the man with a strong right upper cut that sent him staggering back two steps and over the tail gate of the swaying truck. The Scar saw the body hit the road behind the truck and bounce as Dale swerved to avoid the tumbling body. Silhouetted in the light he gave her a tired wave and then turned to grope for his hat and revolver.

Throughout the short fight there had been continued shouts from the cab. The truck had slowed momentarily but when Dale had illuminated it with her headlights it had picked up even more speed. His revolver in hand and hat once again on his head, the Purple Scar decided that hiding no longer mattered. He holstered the gun and stuck his head through the rent in the side of the canvas. He climbed up and stuck a leg through the tear. Turning and grabbing a metal strut he stepped out onto the side of the truck. He reached with his right hand got a new grip then shifted his right leg forward as well. He shifted his grip and crossed his left leg over his right. Now he was just two feet away from the passenger side running board.

Taking a breath, the Scar jumped down onto the running board. He caught himself on the outside mirror mount. Steadying himself the Scar then reached down, twisted the door handle and flung the door wide. He found himself staring into the hooded face of a man trying to bring a gun up. The Scar grabbed the man by the collar and steeling himself against the pain he jerked him hard out of the cab with all his strength. The man flew outward with a yell. The Scar shrugged to one side as the hooded man shot past him and with a scream muffled by his hood he disappeared behind the speeding truck. Throwing himself into the cab, the Purple Scar grabbed at the left hand of the driver who was pointing a gun across his body at the masked avenger. He jerked the gun upward and threw his left elbow into the hooded driver's side. The gun fired upward through the roof of the cab. A twist of the driver's gun hand sent the gun flying onto the dash board where it rattled around before sliding off onto the floor.

The gun's report was shockingly loud. The driver's angry Spanish cursing added to the din. The Scar grabbed the wheel and fought for control. The driver fought back, throwing elbows and clawing at the Purple Scar's face. The truck swayed back and forth as the two struggled. Finally, the Scar got his left foot over the transmission hump and crammed his foot down on top of the driver's accelerator foot. The truck jumped forward. It came perilously close to the sedan leading it before the driver panic braked hard.

The Scar had been hoping for just this move and twisted the steering wheel as far to the left as he could. The truck careened into and through the opposite lane, ran through a picket fence, a hedge and dove over a shallow embankment into some trees.

Dale pulled out fifty yards behind the two vehicles. There was enough light from the widely spaced street lights for her to drive without lights so she did. The sedan and the truck following it moved quickly and made several turns in the following minutes before finally straightening up when they turned onto a busier street. Dale had kept an anxious eye on the figure clinging to the side of the truck. By the time the truck had straightened up heading north the figure had reached the top of the canvas covered truck. As she watched the figure seemed to slide toward the side of the truck then for some unknown reason the figure disappeared through the side of the canvas cover into the rear of the truck. Dale was nonplussed. What was Miles thinking?

Almost immediately she saw the flash of what had to be a gun in the back of the truck. She could see movement in the shadowy interior but could not make out what was happening. There was another flash from the truck bed and the truck's brake lights flashed and it started to slow. Dale knew that secrecy no longer mattered. Biting her lip she reached forward and turned on the headlights. The truck was thrown into bright light. Inside she could see two roughly dressed men. As she watched one man suddenly flew backwards off his feet and through the canvas side covering. He hit the pavement, rolled and disappeared off the shoulder of the road.

Caught in her headlights the truck accelerated once more. Dale stayed as close as she dared. She could see two men in the back of the truck trading blows at close range. Suddenly one of the men was thrown violently backwards out of the truck and into her car's path. Dale braked hard and twisted the wheel. She watched the man's body hit the road and actually bounce as she swerved around it. Her heart in her throat it took a few seconds to realize the figure still moving in the back of the truck was wearing a suit and not a black hood. She saw the disguised avenger give her a quick wave before ducking away from the light.

She breathed easier but only for a second. Moments later the figure climbed through the same tear in the canvas the gunman had just been thrown through and began to climb along the truck's side. Dale swerved over to her right so her headlights illuminated the scene. She watched as the figure made it to the running board, then the passenger door flew open and a hooded man was launched into the air. Dale saw his body hit the side of the road and disappear as she sped past. The Scar dove into the cab and Dale could only watch as the truck now began swerving back and forth in the road. She imagined the terrific struggle going on for control of the vehicle. Then the truck swerved across the road through the yard of a house set back from the road and into a grove of trees.

Dale braked the car and came to a stop in a cloud of dust and blue smoke. The sedan ahead of her also swerved to a stop. Caught in its headlights she saw a door flung open but no one exited. A moment later the door slammed shut and the sedan accelerated away with a squeal of tires. Dale debated only a second before driving across the road and pulling up opposite the grove of trees. She jumped out, automatic in hand just as a figure pushed through the trees. Dale dropped her gun arm to her side and almost sobbed in relief. A rather battered figure with a horrifying face walked toward her holstering a weapon on his hip.

As the Purple Scar reached her Dale shook her head and spoke, "You could have just ridden with me, you know."

The Purple Scar looked over his shoulder at the house where lights were coming on and whispered "We'd better go before we're seen." Taking her arm, he steered her back to the Ford. Climbing behind the wheel Dale drove quickly away. As she did her shell shocked mind was still digesting all the violence she had just seen. After a moment she asked, "Is it like this every time?"

There was a pause as Miles pulled off his mask and stowed it away. He ran his hand through his hair and sighed, "Not always. Though sometimes it's actually worse, I'm afraid." As he rubbed his throbbing forearm he added, "I have to admit I'm getting a little tired of these hooded men. When I find out who the Master of Blackness is, I'm going to have a lot to say to him."

As she steered the Ford back toward Swank Street Dale thought about the Blackness and smiled, "Boy, do I have something to tell you about that."

✛✛✛

The Master of Blackness was livid with anger. He could barely keep from screaming as he addressed the red headed man in front of him, "Five men? How could we lose five men?"

The thin man flinched before answering with an Irish brogue, "T'was the Purple Scar. He was inside Wells' house before we got there. We got Wells in the car but somehow the Purple Scar got onto the truck. He got all our boys and wrecked it."

"But how did he know we were going to take Wells? And why couldn't you stop him. Did you use the Blackness?"

"Aye, I used it myself. It covered the whole house. It should have covered our escape but somehow the Scar saw through it and got onto the truck. He must have the luck of the devil. I thought he was still inside the house when we left."

The Master stood up and began pacing up and down the well-furnished room, "I knew about the Purple Scar. I studied his methods and planned for his intervention. Our plans should have negated his knowledge of the criminal element and his street informants. We have our own men and keep them isolated. And our plan has worked so far. The Purple Scar has barely put in an appearance. Why is he here now?"

His red headed henchman answered tentatively, "Maybe he was out of town before."

The Master stopped and gave the leader of his men a severe look, "No! He's been here all along but for some reason we haven't seen him. He's stayed in the background…waiting. I don't like it. He shows up now… why?"

"I canna say, but we've now lost eight men. Things will go harder now."

The Master of Blackness turned on his number two man, "Why? We still have over a dozen men left."

"Aye, but they've heard the stories about the Purple Scar and losing the men tonight hasn't helped."

"It's your job to keep them in line, Murphy. Remind them that there are fewer men to split the loot with. As soon as the plan is finished I'll see they all get home as rich men. A few more days are all we need."

Murphy nodded, "Aye. I'll speak to them." He turned and left the room. The Master of Blackness threw himself into a wingback armchair and brooded. Things were still going well. This was only a minor setback. He just needed a few more days.

CHAPTER FIFTEEN

"**W**hat do you think it was?" Dale sat across from Doc's desk sipping coffee.

Dale was referring to her description of the strange device she had seen the night before. Doctor Murdock looked thoughtful as he replied, "I think it was the same thing that thief Jake saw at the riot. From his and your descriptions, it's got to be some kind of man-carried tank that disperses whatever causes the Blackness." He shook his head, "The way you say it spread out so quickly from the user it must be some kind of compressed gas. I wish I knew what it was."

"Well, it must be something no one's ever heard of. Who could create something like that?"

Doc emptied his cup and smiled, "Someone with a strong background in chemistry, I'd say. That may help us narrow the field."

Dale set her coffee cup down on Doc Murdock's desk and asked, "Well, what do we do for an encore after last night?"

Doc gave her a weak smile, "Well, on my 'to do' list is a talk with Councilman Paley, check on our telegrams and maybe go look for the place I was held. Any suggestions?"

"It sounds like you'll be busy. I can check on the telegrams, if that will help. Have you looked in on Mr. Manero?"

"That will help, Dale. Yes, I checked and Mr. Manero is doing well. He could probably be sent home soon if I didn't think those hooded goons might still be looking for him."

Dale frowned and lowered her voice, "You're not worried that he'll connect us to 'you know who' are you?"

Murdock thought a moment and shook his head, "He knows I'm a doctor and you're my nurse. He thinks Tommy is an old friend of mine who called us for help. He has no reason to suspect us of anything else. When this is all over he should go back to his life without any suspicions. He'll probably be worried more about paying my bill than anything else."

Dale's mouth dropped open in surprise, "You're not . . ."

Doc smiled and held up a hand, "Of course not. I'm just looking at things from Mr. Manero's point of view." He stood up, "I'm going down to the newspaper and see how they're taking Wells' abduction. I'm also going to talk to Paley. Tell Tommy to hold down the fort while you're out."

A half hour later wearing another mask with the appearance of a middle aged, mustached man, the Scar parked the Ford near the Times building. He entered and crossed the lobby noticing a police detective he recognized speaking to a uniformed security guard. Uniformed police officers had also been outside the main doors as well. The Scar tried to look casual as he strolled across the lobby toward a row of telephone booths. Closeting himself inside one, he lifted up the leather encased directory hanging by a chain from the phone. It took no more than a minute to find the listing for Councilman Paley's law office. He dropped a nickel in the machine, dialed and was quickly connected to Paley. He spoke confidently, "Councilman, my name is Parker. I'm a reporter for the *Chesterfield Sun* and would like to ask you a few questions about the current crisis in Akelton."

Paley answered positively, "Of course, I'm always anxious to co-operate with the Fourth Estate."

Always anxious for publicity, the Scar thought to himself, "Great. Who do you think is behind the crime wave striking Akelton and what do they want?"

There was a pause before Paley answered carefully, "At this point we have no idea who is behind the atrocities taking place here in town. I for one am shocked that our police force has not made more progress in getting to the bottom of this crime wave. It says a lot about the Mayor's administration that our police force is not more efficient."

The Scar shook his head although he had not really expected anything other than campaign slogans. Abruptly he changed the subject, "You are, of course, a licensed attorney and quite conversant with the law. What other qualifications do you have to run for Mayor?"

"I have served on the city council for two years and have detailed knowledge of city functions."

"Yes, I understand you moved to Akelton three years ago."

"Yes, that's correct."

"And where did you move from?"

"Just outside Philadelphia, where I was practicing law."

Now the Scar could get to his real questions, "And where did you study law?"

"At Penn State."

"Good. Let me note that down. And where did you take your undergraduate degree?"

"The same school; I applied directly to law school after I graduated."

"Uh huh, and what did you study there?"

There was pause, "What do you mean?"

"I mean, in what under graduate field did you study? Political Science? History?" A slight pause, "Chemistry?"

"I took a degree in history and graduated near the top of my class."

"I see. And where were you raised? There in Pennsylvania or perhaps somewhere closer to Akelton?"

There was a longer pause, "What kind of question is that?"

"The public might be very interested in your background and early years, Councilman,"

Paley continued in a more official voice, "I'm sure you understand how busy we all are here in Akelton, what with the current crisis. I'm afraid I'll have to cut this short. I have important duties to see to."

"Are you sure? I have many more questions, Councilman."

"Yes, I am. Thank you for your interest." There was click in the Scar's disguised ear and the line went dead. He hung up the phone and thought, "Good. That rattled his cage." He pulled the phone booth door open and walked across the lobby toward the information desk.

Suddenly a loud bell began ringing. He and everyone else stopped and

"And where did you move from?"

looked around. Someone burst though the stairwell door and yelled, "Fire in the basement!"

The Scar broke into a run for the stairwell. Throwing open the door he leaped down the stairs two at a time and crashed through the fire door at the bottom. It was smoky here but the corridor was not yet filled with smoke. Grabbing a handkerchief from his pocket the Scar clapped it over his face and turned right toward where the smoke seemed thickest. He heard shouts behind him as bent over he made his way forward.

He quickly reached a junction. To his right the smoke was thicker. To his left the corridor was filled with Blackness. It was as he suspected, the hooded men were making another attack. What were they after this time? Then he spied a form under the smoke lying in the hallway. Getting down on hands and knees the disguised avenger crawled forward fifteen feet to where a man lay unconscious. Grabbing a hold of the man's jacket he pulled the limp form down the corridor.

At the junction he met armed police officers. They ignored him and plunged down the opposite corridor into the Blackness in pursuit of the hooded men. Behind them came two security guards carrying portable fire extinguishers. They turned into the opposite corridor.

Reaching a point where he could get to his feet the Scar lifted the unconscious man to his shoulder and made his way to the stairwell. He had to fight his way up the stairs past more police heading toward the basement. As he was exiting onto the main floor, from up the stairwell came the sound of distant gunshots. Once in the lobby the Scar laid his burden down. He frowned when he saw that it was the lonely records attendant.

The disguised doctor went quickly to work attempting to revive the man. It was not long before the man gasped, coughed and began draw in deep breaths. While he had been engaged in this effort, firemen and ambulance attendants had flooded the lobby of the newspaper. He gladly turned his patient over to these men and faded away.

Outside in the fresh air the Scar speculated to himself on what the objective of this latest raid had been. More terror certainly; but why the fire? Unless it was an attempt to destroy the newspaper's old files. That would make sense if the Master of Blackness was worried about his past. The Scar was more convinced than ever that the young Sykes boy had returned. The question was; who was he masquerading as?

Reaching his car, the Scar walked past it looking instead for another telephone. He soon found one in a nearby restaurant. In the booth with the door pulled closed the Scar quickly dialed the same number he dialed earlier. Giving a phony name and requesting legal help he was soon connected again with Paley.

"Alan Paley; what can I do for you?"

The Scar lowered his voice and replied to a harsh whisper, "I know you're involved in all this and I'm watching you!"

"What? Who is this?"

"You know who it is!"

There was a quick pause before Paley continued, "Look, I don't know what you're talking about . . ."

"I'll be coming for you soon." The Scar quickly hung up. That should really get Paley looking over his shoulder. He had no direct evidence of the Councilman's involvement with the Blackness, but his instincts were screaming that Paley was up to his neck in the recent trouble. Putting in another nickel, the Scar dialed Swank Street. Tommy answered. When Doc inquired as to how he was Tommy replied, "I'm fine, Doc. A little stiff and this sling gets in the way a bit but other than that I'm okay."

"Good. I have a job for you if you're feeling up to it. I want you to go over to Paley's law office. Get the address out of the phone book. Keep an eye on the place. If he goes anywhere, follow him. When he leaves for the day, follow him to make sure he actually goes home. I know it'll be hard to stay out of sight with that arm but do your best."

"I'll get on it right away, Boss." The Scar then hung up and left the restaurant. He collected the Ford and drove quietly through town keeping an eye out for any trouble but the only thing he noted was the emptiness of the streets and heavy police presence. Once away from downtown he made his way towards the river and headed north.

He started his search on River Road a mile above where it widened into the bay. He drove at a sedate pace looking for the road he had turned out of. It must be on his right; opposite the river. He passed many roads a few paved, many not. Most of them had no names just county road numbers printed on signs at their intersection with River Road.

Eventually The Scar found himself driving up a long shallow grade in the road. He shook his head recognizing the spot. This was where he had been driven over the bluff. Reluctantly admitting that he had missed the road he was looking for the Scar turned his car around and headed south.

Traveling more slowly back over ground he had covered before helped. This time the Scar spotted the road he wanted or at least he thought it was the correct road. Turning, he drove down the road looking for familiar landmarks. It was slow work. Periodically the Scar stopped the Ford to look around. The area around him was mainly planted fields. There were fences alongside the road and scattered farm houses. It felt right but the last time through here he had not had the time to note specific landmarks. He continued on and passed many other gravel roads crossing his. Sometimes he turned and followed a road if it felt right. He drove down several dead end roads and was forced to back track several times. After some time he came to a gravel four way intersection. This looked familiar. He stopped the Ford and got out to look around. The county road sign at the intersection meant nothing to him; they were just numbers. Still he was sure he had come through an intersection like this during the wild chase. The question was which way to go.

The Scar walked to the center of the gravel intersection and stood checking to see how familiar the view looked. He then turned to face another direction and did the same. The third time he repeated this action the view felt right. He quickly looked behind him at the gravel stretching away around a bend. That was the way.

Hopping back in the sedan the Scar turned the car and drove in a new direction. The road wandered back and forth as it wove past tended crops and orchards. Finally on a long stretch of road dominated by a freshly plowed field with a large barn towering in the distance he pulled the Ford to a stop. Here. This was where the car full of hooded men had caught up with him. So, somewhere nearby should be a crossroads to the right. A hundred yards further along and there it was. The Scar turned and followed this new road.

The fields were less tended here and the gravel road in worse shape. The road followed the contours of the land with few landmarks other than fences and the occasional spreading oak tree. He passed an abandoned farmhouse and then a run down but occupied one. He was sure he was close but was unsure about the exact location of the farmhouse he had fled from.

A house set back from the road came into view on his left. He slowed the Ford and looked closely. Then he saw it. Stopping the Ford in the middle of the road the Scar stepped out. A battered, rusty metal mailbox lay next to the fence line along the road. Looking down he could see several pieces of broken wooden post scattered across the gravel. This was the drive he had turned out of and that was the shattered mailbox he had struck. Getting back into his car the Scar turned down the long drive. He drove carefully along the overgrown track, through the low, wet spot and into the yard.

The yard looked just the same. The barn doors still hung wide open and the house and yard were empty. Stepping out the Scar looked carefully around. Consulting the map in his head he decided that he was several miles north of town. He was east of River Road probably three or four miles southeast of where he had reached that road and turned north; a few miles north of there he had been driven over the bank. With a better idea of where he was the Scar walked around to the rear of the house and looked across the fields. Using the sun, he turned slowly in a circle to orient himself with the direction he had come from on foot. Finally he lifted his arm and pointed to a location across the fields at a spot in the distant tree line. About there was where he had left the forest.

Locking the Ford, The Scar set out across the field toward where he thought he had come out of the woods. He waded through thigh high grass. Two hundred yards away he climbed a fence and pushed on through more grass. All this looked familiar and sure enough the Scar soon reached a creek running north and south in front of him and on the other side a line of trees paralleling it. Beyond the trees he could see a distant tree line. Quickly the Scar waded across the creek and pushed uphill through the tall grass toward the heavy woods ahead.

Reaching the edge of the woods he turned and walked along the edge of the trees. Soon enough he found flattened grass indicating something had left the woods at this point and crossed the field. Further along he found more such indications. One of these tracks was certainly his; the others were from his pursuers.

Cautiously the Scar followed one trail into the woods. Immediately he was in deep shadow. He soon found a track running through the woods. He stopped and thought back. He had run through the woods for at least a mile or two along twisting narrow tracks. There had been many crossing paths and he had been totally disoriented. He shook his head; it would be useless to continue. He was comfortable in the woods but he did not have the tracking skills to find his way back to where he had been held. The best thing to do was to get back to town and attempt to find his location with maps of the area. He knew where the farm was. He should be able to track back from there if the maps were detailed enough. He even knew just where to find such maps. The problem was getting to them. He turned and headed back out across the open fields toward his car.

CHAPTER SIXTEEN

Later, back at Swank Street Murdock showered and changed before checking on his patients. He spoke with Mr. Manero. The merchant wanted to get back to his family and Doc reassured him that Dale had gotten word to them that he was alright. Mollified, he agreed to lay low at the clinic for a couple of more days. He actually seemed to believe Doc when he said the police were closing in on the hooded raiders. Doc knew that there wasn't much truth in that but he also felt sure that he was getting closer to solving the mystery of whoever was behind the chaos plaguing Akelton.

Tommy soon returned looking fairly fit. His arm in a sling would be remembered and negate Tommy's ability to blend in. Other than that though, the little man claimed he was none the worse for his brush with the hooded men.

Later over take-out sandwiches Dale had brought in, the three confederates discussed their progress. Tommy reported that he had watched Paley's office and followed the councilman home at close of business. He was ready to go back and continue his watch if Doc wished.

In addition to food, Dale had brought two telegrams that she had picked up that afternoon. One was from Penn State University confirming that Alan Paley was in fact a graduate of that institution with degrees in History and Law. Doc was chagrined. He was sure that Paley was involved somehow with the hooded men. Turning to Tommy, Doc said, "It looks like Paley is a dead end. You might go by and check that he's still at home but don't hang around too long. Then report back here." Tommy nodded his assent.

The other telegram was more interesting. Murdock tore it open, read it then exclaimed, "Hello! This is interesting. It's from our detective friend out in St. Louis. He says that young Sykes did come to stay with cousins there after the death of his father. He graduated high school with good grades a few years later and funded by a small trust fund left for college in Southern Florida. After that Sykes has not had any further contact with his relatives.

Dale raised an eyebrow, "I don't suppose there's much doubt about what he studied is there?"

Doc returned her look, "Chemistry would be my guess. And he seems to have brought his skills back to Akelton seeking revenge."

Tommy swallowed a bite of sandwich and spoke up, "Chemistry? Is that what the Blackness is? Somethin' he cooked it up in a test tube?"

"More like a fully equipped laboratory, I'd say. Sykes probably took a degree in one or more of the sciences and somehow used those skills to develop the Blackness. From what Dale saw the other night it must be some kind of liquid or gas that can be compressed and used from man portable tanks. Tanks that look enough like portable flame throwers to fool our informant from the other night. But you're missing an important point, Tommy."

The little man looked confused, "What's that?"

"Southern Florida isn't that far from Cuba. In fact I believe there are a lot of Cuban immigrants living there."

Tommy snapped his fingers, "You're right, Doc. That's explains why Mr. Manero recognized those hooded guys' accents, they're probably from down south."

As Doc nodded, Dale put in, "But a full laboratory to manufacture this Blackness must take up a lot of space, much less hiding all these Cuban toughs he's working with. Where is he hiding out?"

"I'm not sure…yet. Maybe a look at the maps in the county assessor's office may help."

Dale looked skeptical, "Miles, that office is in one of the guarded buildings downtown. How are you going to get in there on a weekend?"

Doc Murdock stood up with a smile on his face, "I think it's time to give Dan Griffin a call."

Late that night the Purple Scar lifted the window on the second floor at the rear of the county building. Stepping from the fire escape into a darkened hallway he quietly closed the window behind him. Using his flash sparingly he prowled the halls until he found the stairs down to the first floor.

Earlier after they had finished eating, Murdock got Dan Griffin on the phone, "Any news?"

"Nothing new, Miles. There have been some more disruptions around town but we're not sure they aren't just copycat actions. Other than the attack on the *Times* there have been no confirmed uses of the Blackness in any robberies today. What about you?"

"Nothing definite but I may have a clue how to find the hideout of the hooded men. I need your help though."

"Anything you need. What can I do?"

"I need to get into the county office building. I know you have it guarded so I need your help getting in."

"That's easy. I'll send word to have you admitted tomorrow. My men have keys. What do you need there?"

"I need to get into the county assessor's office to look at the plat maps … and tomorrow won't do. I need to get in there tonight."

"What's so important?"

"I may be able to pin down the location where I was held, if I can get a look at those maps. And the sooner I do the better. Also it would look suspicious if I was allowed in there tomorrow, even in disguise. Instead, I would like you to transfer some of the guards to other places tonight. Leave a minimum guard on duty. That will make it easier for me to sneak in and spend some time in the office."

There was a pause as Griffin thought this over, "Alright, I can do that. Let me know what you find."

"I will, thanks Dan." Doc hung up after pledging to be in touch.

Now the Purple Scar was prowling the second floor of the county office building. He met no one and soon found the main stairway downward. Reaching the first floor, he crouched on the stairs and looked through the balusters. Two uniformed police officers were near the locked front door. One sat at the information desk the other leaned on it talking to his partner. When he was sure they were not looking, the Scar slipped off the staircase and down a side hall. Moments later he was standing in front of a door with *Assessor's Office* painted on the frosted glass upper half.

The door opened on the second try of one of his master keys and the Scar slipped inside locking the hall door behind him. He flashed his light around just long enough to see the inner door he was looking for. This door was unlocked and he entered the windowless room and closed the door behind him.

This good sized room was filled with wall to wall shelves. The shelves were filled with leather bound books many of them very large. Using his pocket flash, the Scar bypassed the birth, death and marriage records and went straight to the very large plat map books. It took a few minutes to find the right one. Lifting it down he placed the heavy leather bound book on a table in the center of the room. The Scar flipped it open and leafed through the oversize pages until he came to the one he wanted.

Orienting himself he ran his finger along River Road. He found the side road he wanted and traced his path as well as he could. A minute later he reached what he was sure was the abandoned farm where he had borrowed the truck. Unfortunately it was near the edge of the page and he could not trace his path through the woods. Turning the page he found his place and quickly traced the contours of the map with a gloved finger. He stopped and punched the paper hard with that finger. Nodding, he traced a path to other roads and muttered in a low breath, "Now, that is interesting."

Noting down the plat number of a particular parcel, the Purple Scar closed the book and replaced it on a shelf. He then left the record room and re-entered the main office and drifted silently across the office to a bank of file cabinets. The building was still silent so he used his flash briefly to locate the cabinet and drawer he wanted. He was just opening the file drawer when something caught his attention out of the corner of his eye.

Through the frosted upper half of the main office door a light appeared. The Scar slid the file drawer closed and ducked down behind a desk. A moment later the sound of someone rattling the door knob came to his ears. Thankful he had re-locked the door behind him, the Scar remained motionless until footsteps had receded down the hall.

Moving back to the file cabinet he resumed his search. Minutes later he found the information he wanted. The Scar paused and gave a quiet but triumphant chuckle. He was sure he had found the hooded men's hideout. He was also now certain that the Sykes boy had returned and most importantly thought he knew who he was masquerading as.

The Scar closed the drawer and ghosted back to the hallway door. Listening he heard nothing. Unlocking the door he cautiously stuck his head out. A quick inspection of the hallway showed it empty. It took only a moment for him to re-lock the door behind him and drift down the hall toward the rear of the building. Minutes later the Scar was ducking through the same second floor window he had entered. He closed it behind him and quietly climbed down the fire escape and dropped into the deserted alley. The side street at the end of the alley was quiet. The squad car that had been there earlier in the evening had been re-called at Dan Griffin's order. The Purple Scar turned onto the sidewalk and walked quietly away.

+++

Back at Swank Street, Murdock found Tommy waiting up for him. Dale had gone home to her apartment.

"How did it go, Doc?"

"Actually very good, Tommy. I think we finally have the break we need. I know where to find the hooded men and I know who is leading them."

"Really?' That's great! When do we go after them?"

Doc smiled, "Slow down. Tomorrow will be soon enough. There are plans to be made. Now tell me, did you get Paley tucked in?"

Tommy face lit up, "That's the thing Doc. He's up to something. I went back to his apartment and watched it. About ten o'clock the lights went out and I figured he had gone to bed. I was just leaving when he comes out the front door. I was surprised and slipped into an alley to watch. He looked around and walked to the corner. He just stood there for a while like he was waiting for something so I tried to get a little closer. After about five minutes a car pulls up and Paley jumps in the back. I rushed up there but before I could get close the car had disappeared. I'm sorry, Doc. Paley's up to something fishy and I lost him."

Doc took this surprising information in stride, "That's alright Tommy. At least this confirms Paley is involved in something shady. You'd better get some rest now."

"What about you, Doc?"

"I have some thinking to do."

CHAPTER SEVENTEEN

Doctor Murdock was up early checking on Mr. Manero. After that he and Tommy ate a quick breakfast upstairs in his apartment. He was just piling dishes into the sink in his kitchen when he heard Dale's voice in the hallway talking to Tommy. She walked into the kitchen carrying a folded newspaper and looking upset. Before Doc could ask what was wrong she handed him the newspaper. Unfolding it, the front page headline screamed at him, "Mayor Kidnapped!"

Doc shook his head. Dale spoke, "So you haven't heard? It's all over the radio this morning. I'm surprised Dan Griffin hasn't called." Before Murdock could respond, the telephone rang. He moved quickly into his study to answer it. Griffin was on the other end of the line, "I suppose you've heard the latest news by now."

"Just now. What are the details?"

Griffin's voice sounded tired, "A crew of the hooded men attacked the mayor's home very late last night. We had men guarding the place but they used that damned Blackness to cover their attack. In the confusion they got away with him. His wife wasn't hurt but one of our patrol officers was killed and another wounded. On the plus side we killed another hooded man and we're sure more were wounded in the gunfight."

Miles queried, "Anything on the dead body?"

"No, although he looked a lot like the others we've found. They all have very dark hair and complexions. The coroner is certain they are all of the same ethnic type."

"Yes. I believe they are Cuban in origin; either ex-patriots living in South Florida or from Cuba itself."

Griffin was silent for a moment before demanding, "What do you know?"

"I'm finally getting a handle on this mess, Dan. Everything leads to Florida."

"Florida? What the devil has Florida got to do with the Blackness?"

"Do you remember the Sykes suicide and scandal fifteen years ago?"

Doc could hear the line hum during Griffin's thoughtful pause, "Yes, I was still a patrol sergeant back then. I didn't answer that call but I know officers who did. A terrible tragedy. Sykes had been ruined financially and committed suicide. He left his little boy an orphan."

"That's right. I've done a lot of research and I'm convinced that the young Sykes boy has returned for revenge. Somehow he is behind the Blackness and the hooded men."

"What? How can that be?"

"My research so far indicates that there were four men involved in Sykes' business troubles: Darlan, MacPherson, Bannerman and Russo."

There was another pause as Griffin digested this news. Finally he said with a sigh, "I don't suppose that could be a coincidence, could it?"

"I'm afraid not. I've traced the Sykes boy through Missouri and finally to Florida. That gives us a possible connection with these Cubans. Somehow he created this Blackness or perhaps stole it. I'm convinced he has returned with these Cubans and the Blackness to wreak his revenge on the four men who ruined his father and Akelton as well."

"Alright, I'm not sure I follow all of your connections, Miles but if you're right, how do we find him?"

"If I'm right he is hiding in plain sight, masquerading as an upright citizen right here in town."

"What? Who?"

"I've got a pretty good idea who but I need a few more hours to confirm it. And there is Wells and the Mayor to think about now. We have to be careful. Can you have a flying squad of men standing by tonight?"

"I certainly can. I'll be at Headquarters, you can reach me there."

"Good. Wait for my call. I'll call you as soon as I'm sure where to send your men. " The two friends said their goodbyes and hung up. Murdock turned to Dale and she said, "You know who is behind this now, don't you? Why not tell Dan?"

Doc let a long breath, "He'll know soon enough. You're going to drive me to their hideout tonight when it's dark. I need to get out there first and try to get Wells and the Mayor to safety…if they're still alive. After that Dan can send in the troops." He gave Dale a weak smile before adding, "With luck this will all be over by tomorrow." Doc then walked across the room to his concealed wall safe. Opening it, he removed a newly made mask and secreted it away inside his jacket. He also gathered up his master keys and revolver. Finally he turned to Dale and said, "Keep an eye on our patients. I need to go out and check on one last thing."

Dale smiled weakly and nodded as Doc turned and left by the back stairs.

In the black Ford with his new innocent-appearing mask in place, the Scar motored across town to a two story brick building three blocks up from City Hall. The humid heat wave continued but today the sky looked different. Dark clouds were building up to the west. The air felt even heavier. Doc felt the change in the air. He knew thunderstorm weather when he saw it. Those dark clouds were building up into thunderheads that climbed thousands of feet high. They would eventually bring rain and relief from the muggy heat. The only question was when.

One good thing about all the attacks by the Cubans was that people were staying off the streets. Despite the heavy police presence just a few blocks over, the side street where the Scar parked was deserted. The Scar got out of his car, looked around and ghosted into the alley. Behind the brick building he easily located the rear door and went to work on it with his master keys. Within a minute he had it open.

Inside on the ground floor the Scar worked his way thorough hallways to the front of the building. The office just off the lobby was locked and the Scar was just reaching for his master keys again when he spied some paperwork sitting on a side table. Interested, he sorted through the various folders and picked one out. He read through it quickly. He set it down when he was finished and smiled to himself. The information he was looking for was right there in front of him. The Scar quickly turned and made his way out of the building. He relocked the alley door and walked quietly to the alley's entrance. The street was still deserted and moments later the Scar was driving away in the nondescript Ford. Twenty minutes later he was entering the alley behind Swank Street.

Murdock found Dale in the apartment's kitchen fixing sandwiches for lunch. Doc greeted her there, "I'll take over here. I have something for you to do." He handed her a piece of paper, "I need you to call this organization and ask them that question." Dale read the paper with surprise, "You know that it's Saturday and everything is closed, Don't you?"

"I do, and I don't care. Get a hold of the chancellor, the Dean, the President for all I care; get them at home if you have to. This is the final confirmation and we need it today."

Dale nodded thoughtfully and handed him the kitchen knife she was holding. Taking the paper she turned to leave but stopped, "Is it really him?" The knife in his hand Doc nodded, "It looks like it. We just need the final confirmation." Dale nodded and left the room as Doc turned back to the counter.

He made sandwiches and took them to Tommy who in turn took some food into Mr. Manero. Murdock then made sandwiches for Dale and himself, He took hers into his study where Dale sat at his desk talking heatedly into the phone, "I don't care who you have to get hold of. I told you this is a matter of life and death! We need that information today! Yes. Yes, I'll be at this number. Thank you." Dale hung up the phone and glared at him. "Bureaucracy! Don't people understand the term emergency?" Doc set a plate and glass of milk in front of her and smiled, "I'm sure you got your point across." Dale's glare dissolved into a smile and from there quickly turned into laughter.

Two hours later the phone rang. Doc hung back and let Dale run into his study to answer it. He lounged in the doorway listening.

"Yes, this is she...uh, huh...you're sure? No, that's all we really needed. Thank you, you've been very helpful. I appreciate you calling me on Saturday. Yes, good bye." Dale hung up the phone and frowned. Doc lifted an eyebrow at her but said nothing. Finally Dale spoke, "You were right. They've never heard of him. No record at all." Finally Dale said, "So it's him just as you suspected."

Doc nodded, "Well, he's involved somehow...deeply involved, I just don't know how, yet. But so is Paley. I intend on finding out the truth tonight."

Dale bit her lower lip for an instant before shaking her head, "I wish you would get some help from Dan. You're going to be outnumbered worse than you've ever been."

"I have to do this alone." He paused before adding, "There's a chance I can get the Mayor and Wells out…if they're still alive, but I have to go in alone."

Dale walked around the desk to stand in front of him. She lowered her voice, "Something's different this time." She looked at her tall fiancé and for a moment before saying, "Somehow this is personal now."

Doc nodded, "I'm not sure when it happened. Maybe when I was nearly killed out on River Road, maybe ever since that first night during the riot when I nearly thought I'd lost you. I'm not sure why but there's something different about this madness. I need to go out there and settle it myself."

Seeing the worried look on Dale's lovely face Doc tried to lighten the mood, "Hey, you'll be with me. I trust you to bring Dan and his men in when I need them. He'll be standing by for your call."

Dale thought for a moment before nodding, "Okay, but Tommy won't like being left behind."

"No, but that's the way it has to be. We'd better start getting ready. We should leave with plenty of time to spare."

Dale stood up, "Right."

CHAPTER EIGHTEEN

Dale and Doc left by the secret alley door and exited in the next block over. Dale took the wheel of the Ford. Doc sat next to her checking his equipment. Dale had been right; Tommy had not liked being left behind. Doc had had to point out, "With that arm in a sling you can't drive, Tommy. I hate to leave you here but what if some fast driving is called for? You can't shift and steer with only one hand."

Tommy had looked crestfallen but finally agreed, "Just be careful Doc, and take care of Dale, will ya."

"I always do."

Dale pulled the Ford onto the street and drove casually through the lightly traveled streets headed north through town. All afternoon the clouds had built and by sunset the sky was already dark with masses of gray and black clouds. An ominous rumble of thunder came to their ears as they sat at an intersection waiting for the traffic light to change.

"Somehow this is personal now."

Simultaneously a breeze sprang up and cool air blew through the open windows of the sedan. Dale commented, "The hot spell is finally breaking."

"Yes, we're in for a change. We'll have some nasty thunderstorms tonight."

Dale glanced his way, "Won't that make things more dangerous?"

"Perhaps, but it could also give me cover. Thunder and lightning make good diversions."

Dale nodded as the light changed and she accelerated through the intersection.

As the pretty nurse navigated her way quietly through town, Murdock checked the load in his revolver and re-holstered it. He had brought plenty of extra cartridges, hoping he would not need them. His fearsome purple mask was secreted in its hidden pocket inside his jacket. His pants pockets contained both his pencil flash and his trusty master keys. Satisfied that everything was ready, he pulled on a pair of lightweight, black leather gloves and rested his hands in his lap.

He sat quietly as Dale passed through mid-town and continued north. He said nothing; Dale knew very well, exactly where they were going. Soon they were away from the built up area of Akelton and driving through streets lined with two story buildings of businesses and apartments. Soon they picked up a main street that headed north. Minutes later larger buildings had thinned out and the street had become a main road leading north out of town. They stayed with this road for several minutes longer then turned left onto a major country road. The road was very dark with only lights from homes and farms set back from the road to be seen. Thunder rumbled in the distance.

At the next intersection, Dale hesitated for a moment before turning right and heading northwest. Doc nodded imperceptibly; she remembered. Minutes later she slowed and began looking left and right as she spoke in a low voice, "Shouldn't it be around here, somewhere?"

Doc straining for the sight of a landmark along his side of the road replied, "We're close."

At that moment came a momentary flash of distant lightning. In the strobe like flash, Doc saw a large house set well back from the road on his right. "I remember that house. I think it's only a half mile or so along this road."

Dale nodded and fed power to the sedan. A minute later, lights illuminated the darkened road. Headlights coming down a hill from the right paused at the road and then turned toward the Ford. Doc ducked down and whispered, "Keep going. Don't slow." Dale obeyed as a canvas covered truck passed them headed southeast the way they had just come. After it had passed Dale whispered, "That looked just like the truck the other night!"

Sitting up and looking over his shoulder through the rear window of the Ford, Doc replied, "I'm sure it was. And it came out of the right drive. Turn around quick!"

Dale twisted the steering wheel and slowed the car. She then put it in reverse and cranked the steering wheel the other way. While she was turning the sedan, Doc Murdock was rubbing his chin, "That's almost surely a bunch of hooded men headed into town to make trouble."

Now straightened up in the road, Dale accelerated after the truck, "We have to stop them."

Much as he wanted to disagree, Doc knew that Dale was right. If that truck was full of hooded men headed into town they would no doubt be kidnapping more innocent people, blowing up statues or causing who knows what kinds mayhem. In any case, they had to be stopped. So even though they had been on The Master of Blackness' doorstep, Doc told his fiancé, "Step on it. We have to keep them in sight while I think of something."

Dale did just that and sped up. There came another flash of lightning just as they reached the nearest intersection and the truck was nowhere to be seen. She wrenched the sedan to the left without being told. Seconds later the rumble of the accompanying thunder came to their ears. Minutes later they reached the main road leading back toward Akelton. To their right they could see the headlights of the truck going toward town. Doc pointed, "Follow it, but don't get too close."

Dale did as she was ordered and pulled onto the main road leading into Akelton. She closed the distance until they were cruising behind the canvas covered truck perhaps fifty yards back.

Canvas covered the rear of the truck so they could not see what cargo the truck carried but Doc was sure it was trouble. Gripping the wheel with white knuckles Dale asked, "Couldn't we get ahead somehow, find a phone and call Dan? Let him know the raiders are coming?"

Murdock thought a moment before shaking his head "Just knowing they were coming wouldn't do any good. We don't know what their target is tonight. I would have to stop the truck and somehow keep them occupied while you get help. Meanwhile they could scatter and I'd be tied up here in town chasing hooded men when I need to be back at the mansion searching for the Mayor." Dale saw the sense in this but didn't like it, "What do we do then?"

Doc was at a loss himself when he saw the brake lights of the truck flash. They were reaching the built up area near the edge of town. An intersection with stop signs all four ways was ahead. Here the road widened and there was a center turn lane. Inspiration suddenly struck the physician, "There! Pull up next to the truck at that stop sign! Hurry!"

Pulling out his mask Doc quickly slipped its horrifying features down over his face. As the truck pulled to a stop at the four way intersection; Dale pulled into the turn lane and drifted up beside it. The Purple Scar spoke quickly, "I'm taking the truck. When I leave, get into town and call Griffin. I need a half hour. Got it? A half hour from now!"

Dale slowed the sedan to a stop and the Scar was out the door in a flash. Two steps and he jumped to the running board on the driver's side of the cab, one hand reaching for his revolver. Inside a red haired man in a leather jacket sat calmly behind the wheel. Startled by the sudden appearance of someone on his running board he turned and stared directly into the horribly frightening disfigured face of John Murdock, the murdered brother Miles Murdock had sculpted the mask from. The driver's mouth opened but his power of speech was paralyzed just long enough for the Scar to wrench open the door and grab hold of the collar of his leather jacket. With one mighty pull he jerked the man outward as he slammed his revolver butt into the man's face. The Scar then leaned to one side as the stunned man flew past him to bounce off the grill of the Ford and landed in the street in front of the surprised Dale.

The Scar jumped behind the wheel just as another flash of lightning lit the sky. He eased the door closed and its metallic click was swallowed up by the rumble of the following thunder. There came a loud, questioning shout from the back of the truck but it was in Spanish. The Scar ignored it as he shoved the truck into gear and revved the engine. He twisted the wheel and made a right turn. The truck's motion seemed to have settled any questions from the back. The Scar smiled to himself. Now it was time to take these gentlemen for a ride. He made another right turn at the next street, headed back north.

+++

Dale was totally unprepared for the Scar's quick movement. Her mouth opened but her words caught in her throat as she saw the trim form of the masked avenger jump onto the running board of the truck. The next thing she knew a red haired man had bounced off the Ford's grill and disappeared in front of the sedan. She sat stunned as the truck, now under new control turned right and drove west. It turned left immediately at the next street and disappeared somewhere behind her.

She let out her breath and started to smile when a groan came to her ears. Then a shaking hand appeared over the hood and grabbed hold of one headlight. Shakily, a roughly dressed red haired man, blood on his face, pulled himself to his feet leaning heavily on the hood. Dale was nonplussed for a moment. Then she quickly let in the clutch and immediately pushed it in again. This caused the Ford to lurch forward a foot. It was just enough to throw the groaning man onto his back in the street.

Dale scrabbled in her purse and came up with her .32. She jumped out of the car and carefully rounded front bumper, her pistol up. The man was lying in the street unconscious. Dale had not rolled over him; she had just thrown him off the bumper. He must have hit his head on the road. She knelt and carefully felt for a pulse. The freckle faced man was alive but unconscious. Dale breathed a sigh and stood up frowning. Now what was she going to do. A car pulled up at the intersection across from her and a man got out. He yelled across, "Are you alright?"

Thinking quickly, Dale concealed the gun behind her back and waved, "I'm fine but this man needs help."

The stranger jogged across the intersection. Dale stepped back and quickly shoved her pistol under the front seat. She then met the stranger in front of her car.

He asked, "What happened?"

Dale held up her hands and tried to look confused, "I pulled up at the stop sign and as I started across the intersection, he ran out in front of me. I was barely moving but he was knocked down. I don't believe he's badly hurt but he needs to get to a doctor. Can you help me?"

"Of course, Miss. What do you want to do?"

"I'm a nurse. If we can get him in my car I can drive him to a hospital to be checked over. I can also call the police from there."

The stranger nodded, "Right, let's get him in your car." He lifted the man's shoulders while Dale grabbed the gunman's legs. Between the two of them they managed to get the unconscious Cuban into the Ford's back seat. Another driver had stopped during all this but Dale politely declined any more help. With the unconscious gunman safely in her back seat she thanked the passing motorist and was soon behind the steering wheel and driving into town again. Her pistol was on her lap and her mind was on finding Dan Griffin before her passenger woke up. She glanced at her watch as she pushed the accelerator down. She was on a schedule now.

The Scar wrestled the truck off the main road and onto the well maintained county road he and Dale had traversed less than twenty minutes before. He soon made the right turn onto the final road as he neared his destination. Then came a loud call in Spanish from the back of the truck. "Uh, oh," he thought. It sounded as if his passengers were getting restless. He ignored the voice and kept the accelerator down.

Moments later he had almost reached his destination. There was now persistent shouting coming from the back of the truck but the Scar wasn't worried. They were very near the end of their journey. The truck's headlights picked up the twin brick pillars marking the drive he was looking for. As the truck swept past the drive the Scar wrenched the steering wheel hard to the left. As he did he opened the driver's door and put one foot on the running board. The truck was now headed across the narrow county road directly for some heavy undergrowth. Satisfied the Scar stepped off the running board. As his feet hit the ground he curled into a ball and rolled way from the runaway truck. He came to a stop sprawled in the middle of the road just in time to see the truck plunge into some heavy bushes on the other side. He was surprised when it tipped forward and disappeared from sight with the sounds of cracking limbs and tearing bushes.

As the Scar got to his feet brushing dust from his jacket there came a bang and crash of metal as the truck hit something solid below. As he turned away he thought idly that there must have been a bigger drop off at the side of the road than he had thought.

The Scar didn't need to see his watch in the darkness to know he was running short of time. As he jogged past the brick gate posts he didn't even glance at the brass plaque affixed to one of them. Instead he concentrated on making good time as he jogged up the long gravel drive. A hundred yards up the drive widened. With the heavy overcast blocking any moonlight, the Scar had to depend on infrequent lightning flashes to see ahead. As he did he noticed that the accompanying thunder was following closer on the heels of the lightning.

At this point the Scar moved left and into the trees. Using this cover he skirted the wide open area in front of the mansion. When he was directly opposite the portico he crept forward until he found a place where he could see the front of the three-story building clearly. There were a few lights burning on the first floor. There were more on the second floor and none on the third floor. As he watched a man with a rifle in his arms walked around the left side of the mansion into his vision. The guard appeared to be bored and strolled casually around the front of the mansion and along the gravel drive.

Keeping inside the trees, the Scar paralleled his path. As the guard walked around to the northwest side of the mansion, he saw him turn alongside the mansion and angle toward a very large carriage house. He counted five large doors facing him, all closed. Running the length of the building above the closed vehicle doors were a row of windows, many of them lit from within. Alongside the shorter side of the carriage house was an external set of stairs. The guard climbed the stairs and entered the second floor.

It would make sense that the carriage house was now the mansion's garage. It was perfect for hiding vehicles like covered trucks. Lightning flashed and in the brief moment of illumination the Scar could see the wide gravel path continued past the carriage house and through the trees. Curious he moved that way, staying just inside the trees on this side of the gravel. Fifty yards further on the gravel branched. A narrow path barely four feet wide continued on to the left while a wider path branched directly away from him.

Leaning carefully out the Scar saw no one within sight. He quickly made his way across the gravel and followed the wide path before him. It wound through the trees slightly. He slowed in the darkness as a darker shape loomed up before him. It was large enough to be a building. He could not get a good idea of its size or shape in the shadowy woods. He was about to chance a quick flash of his light when lightning lit the sky.

The brief flash of light showed him a building perhaps fifteen feet tall. The side in front of him was thirty feet across. Large double doors closed off the left side of the front, while a small man sized door was near the right front corner. The Scar approached the building as the accompanying thunder rumbled through the night air. Shielding the beam of his flashlight with his hand he flashed it over the large double doors. They were held together with a brand new padlock and chain. Likewise the construction of the wooden building was also new. He could still detect a faint smell of new wood. His interest piqued, the Scar moved to the smaller door. He pulled out his master keys and went to work. The lock was new and it took five tries before he found a key that turned in the lock.

Inside the Scar closed the door behind him and turned on his pocket flash. The building consisted of one large room approximately thirty feet by twenty five feet. On the side he was standing in a bench ran from front to back along the side wall. It was covered in chemical apparatus. Glass jars, retorts, mixing bowls, Bunsen burners and thermometers cluttered the surface of the bench. At the back facing him the Scar could see large metal barrels, some with labels on them. Under the bench were large cloth sacks and some metal bins. Across from the bench was a raised platform. Metal piping ran from the floor to a set of burners under the platform and atop it was a huge metal cauldron.

Undoubtedly this was where the Blackness was manufactured. And this was also where it was stored thought the Scar as he flashed his light to the left side of the building. There facing the door but set back six feet from it was a huge metal pressure tank. It gleamed in the light from his flash. It was cylindrical in shape and lay on its side. Metal frames under it kept the huge cylinder in place.

A fixture on the front of the cylinder drew his interest. Close examination showed it to be a pressure regulated valve closed by a small spoked wheel. No doubt this was where the man sized packs were filled from the stored Blackness. The Scar marveled at the size of the tank wondering how much chemical it could hold. His thoughts were quickly drawn back to reality when he looked at his watch in the flash's glare. Time was running short. He would have to move fast now. He moved toward the door but stopped in his tracks as a thought came to him.

Pocketing his flash, the Scar boldly exited through the small door and walked to the large double doors. Here he went to work again with his trusty master keys. Pulling the chain loose from the doors he cast both lock and chain into the nearby trees. He then pulled the doors wide open. A flash of lightning illuminated the interior of the building momentarily. Walking back inside, the Scar searched the work bench until he found what he was looking for; a heavy pipe wrench.

The Scar walked back to the huge tank. Taking a breath he twisted wide open the screw valve. As soon as he began turning the spoked wheel, a cloud of Blackness spewed from the open valve under pressure. Lifting the wrench he brought it down hard into the darkness where he knew the valve to be. He couldn't see his blows hit the open valve but he could feel them connect solidly. Dropping the wrench the Scar then back pedaled through the impenetrable Blackness. In seconds he broke into the clear.

The shadowy gravel path seemed bright after the total Blackness. Turning the Scar jogged back to the main path and turned toward the carriage house and mansion. He thought briefly about exploring the smaller path that ran the other way, but he was sure what he would find there. Eventually it would lead to the wooden shack he had been held in four days before. Reaching the cleared area around the carriage house, the Scar worked his way around behind it so he could approach the mansion from the rear. He had seen the front was too brightly lit there to affect an entrance. Also armed guards walked that area.

There was an external stairs on this side of the carriage house as well. Moving silently through trimmed grass, the Scar quickly moved around behind the long building. There he jogged quickly to its far side. From there he could see the rear and near side of the mansion. There was a side door on this side of the mansion but the windows on each side of it were lit. Several windows were lit on the second floor as well. At the rear of the building, four steps led to a large covered porch. There was a rear door here. This would have been perfect for the Scar's purposes if the rear porch had not been brightly illuminated by a light above the door. He moved on behind the mansion keeping to the edge of the trees where he could easily take cover if any wandering guards appeared.

Stealthily the Scar worked his way around to where he could see the opposite side of the mansion. Before he could get a detailed look at this side, he was forced to duck into the tree line as an armed guard came walking along the gravel drive in front of the house. The Scar reached back and put his hand on his revolver as the guard suddenly stopped. A moment later there was the flare of a match as the guard lit a cigarette. The Scar breathed easier as the guard continued his rounds seconds later.

From his position just inside the trees, the Scar studied the mansion. This side of the mansion seemed featureless except for windows. Several appeared to be open for ventilation but even the first floor windows were seven feet above the ground. He was considering his options when it occurred to the masked avenger that the first floor could only be so high if it had a very tall basement. Looking closely the Scar could make out what he thought were dark openings in the foundation along the ground. More importantly there appeared to be a structure attached to the base of the foundation near the rear of the building. An obliging flash of lightning lit the scene momentarily. The structure against the mansion's foundation was clearly an angled concrete basement entrance. To the rumble of the accompanying thunder, the Scar ghosted across the surrounding lawn to the base of the mansion. The angled structure held a double door entrance to the cellar. The doors were sturdy wood set into concrete and angled about thirty degrees up from the horizontal. They were secured with a padlock.

In the shadowy darkness, the Scar knelt and pulled out his master keys. He soon had the padlock opened. He flipped back the hasp and looped the padlock through the eyelet and relocked it. That way no one could relock the door after him. Standing up the Scar gave one of the doors a heave and prayed it was well oiled. It came open silently just as another lightning flash showed a set of concrete steps leading downwards. His revolver in one hand and pocket flash in the other, the Scar descended eight steps into almost total darkness. He flashed the light briefly and saw he was in a deserted basement. Pocketing the flash he turned and quietly closed the door above him.

The basement was hot and stuffy. Flashing his light around he could see the walls were of brick. His attention was drawn immediately to a dim glow to his right. At the rear of the basement a large metal, hot air furnace occupied the entire corner. The glow was coming from behind a grate near the floor. His light showed hot air ducts running out in all directions along the ceiling of the basement. During the winter the ducts would carry hot air throughout the old mansion to warm the rooms. Even in summer the furnace was kept going, probably to provide hot water to the building. Between the furnace and the outside cellar doors was a large wooden coal bin.

The other rear corner held a large sink and a quite modern clothes washer. Next to the washer stood a large canvas cart on wheels; inside were soiled sheets. When he flashed his light behind the cart, the masked avenger saw a horizontal metal laundry chute that quickly angled up and disappeared into the ceiling leading to the upper floors. Near the laundry chute, a narrow set of stairs with a ninety degree bend to the left led to the first floor.

A wall running from one side of the building to the other walled off the rear of the basement from the front half of the building. Two closed doors penetrated this wall. Flipping a mental coin the Scar tried the door on his left. It was locked. He didn't have to try his master keys; a key hung in the lock. He shrugged and turned the key, his gun at the ready. Darkness yawned at him. He chanced a quick flash of his light and found a narrow corridor leading toward the front of the house. It ran fifteen feet and ended in another door. To his right was a blank wall. The left side was much more interesting. Three metal doors locked by large, external bolts lined the left wall.

Moving to the first door the Scar found the door opened outward. An opening at eye height was covered by a small sliding, metal door. Sliding it to one side he saw only darkness. Beaming his light into the small opening he saw a man in trousers and soiled dress shirt sitting in a corner on the floor. Before he held up an arm to shield his eyes from the flashlight's beam, the Scar made out the features of Mayor Morningham.

Nodding to himself, the Scar slid the covering closed and moved to the next door. Sliding the cover open he flashed his light within and saw a brown haired man curled in the corner apparently asleep. He couldn't be certain but it appeared to be Wells the newspaper editor. He slid the cover closed and moved to the third door. This cell appeared to be empty. The Scar threw the bolt back and pulled the door open. Shining his light around, he found a featureless, windowless cell about five feet by eight feet. Chillingly there appeared to be dried blood stains on the floor.

Exiting the third cell the Scar closed the door and glanced at his watch in the beam of his flash. His time was almost up. If Dale had gotten hold of Griffin then police would soon be rolling up the drive. The mayor looked in good enough shape to walk. Wells was unconscious. He probably could get them both safely to the woods but if they were seen by a wandering guard, he would have to shoot it out and hope the captives could get away in the darkness. Plus the Master of Blackness might get away in the confusion. On the other hand, if he had a gun in his face he probably wouldn't be too interested in harming his captives and it would be hard to run away. Besides, after all that had happened, the Scar very much wanted a few words with the man behind all this mayhem.

His mind set, the Scar tried the door at the other end of the hallway. It was locked. He tried his master keys but realized there was a key already in the lock. Just as with the door he had opened. He shrugged and moved back out into the rear of the basement, removing the hall key as he went. He pocketed the key and tried the other door in the front wall. It was unlocked. A quick flash of his light showed a large room set up as workshop. There were several pieces of antique furniture obviously undergoing restoration. Toward the center of the room was a staircase leading up. From its location he decided it probably led to the hall near the front door.

A distant shout caused the Scar to douse his light. Dim light came through high basement windows set along the wall to his right. Avoiding equipment and furniture he walked quickly to stand under a window. The window was closed but he could still hear someone shouting in Spanish. The man was quickly answered by another shout in the same language. Both voices sounded excited. So the spreading Blackness had been noticed; or perhaps some survivors from the truck crash across the road had made their way back to report. Either way the Scar knew he had nearly run out of time.

He turned and hustled across to the rear corner of the basement. In the dark, gun drawn he crept up the narrow stairwell. It ended at a closed wooden door. Listening at it he heard nothing and no light showed underneath. He twisted the door knob and pushed the door open. He found himself standing in a small shelf lined pantry. Dim light came through a small, high window. Another door led out, probably into the kitchen or back entryway the Scar guessed.

Seeing no light under this outer door, he boldly threw it open and led with his gun. He found himself in a large, darkened kitchen. What light there was came from two large curtained windows. From what little he could make out it looked like the kitchen had been restored to as it had been in earlier days. Across the room to his right he pushed open a swinging door and edged an eye around the door jamb. A hallway stretched forward toward the front of the mansion. To his right was a darkened stairway leading up. Most of the first floor was dark. The exception was a pool of light illuminating the front hall and entry way.

At that moment the front door was thrown open and a man dressed in working clothes dashed in. He didn't bother closing the door behind him but rushed for the wide stairway to the upper floors. He was shouting in Spanish as he went. Yes, the alarm had been raised…but for what?

The Scar drifted quietly across the hallway to the narrow rear stairs. They were dark but there was dim light coming from the next floor. Six feet up the stairs bent back upon themselves at a small landing. He took the stairs quietly keeping his steps near the wall to minimize the chances of loose treads squeaking. Seconds later he arrived at the second floor. The Scar stopped and leaned into the hallway. To his right light was coming around a corner of the hallway. To his left was a hallway that turned at right angles and ran somewhere across the rear of the house the Scar guessed. This rear hallway was very dark. Next to the stairwell, about three feet off the ground was a closed door nearly three feet square. A handle protruded at one side of it.

The Scar decided it had to be a dumb waiter or the laundry chute. From its position he guessed it was the latter and led directly to the basement. Marking its location for future reference, he got down on his hands and knees, took off his fedora edged an eye around the corner of the hallway. Looking toward the front of the house he saw a long, wide corridor. It was illuminated only by light coming from two wide open doorways on the left side and a half open door halfway down the corridor on the right side. The Scar could feel the rumble of nearby thunder rattling the old mansion. As he watched the same roughly dressed man he had seen a minute before stepped into the hallway from a door on the right and trotted quickly toward the front of the house.

Replacing his hat on his head, the Scar stood up and crept silently around the corner to the first open doorway. It was an arched opening at least four feet wide. Hearing nothing he poked his head gently around the corner. The large room was empty. It looked like much of the center of this floor had been opened up into an exhibit room. Indirect light came from two shielded wall lights. These illuminated glass-covered display cases and pieces of antique furniture and equipment. The walls were covered with framed black and white photographs, some of them enlarged, as well as paintings. Another wide doorway opened on to this same corridor toward the front of the house. A darkened doorway was directly across the room.

The Scar turned and moved silently up the corridor toward the half open doorway. He had almost reached it when a telephone rang from inside the room. He froze and listened. A voice he couldn't quite make out spoke angrily in what sounded like Spanish; then went silent after a few moments. Moving forward the Scar reached the door. He heard movement, then scraping that sounded like a chair pushed across wood. He shoved the door open with his left hand stepped into the room.

The room was a lavishly appointed study. A decorative fireplace was to his left near two comfortable looking wingback chairs. To his right was a wall of books. The far wall was broken by narrow French doors that opened onto a tiny railed balcony. The doors were open and the curtains were stirred by a strong breeze. The rumble of thunder came through the doors. Ahead, past an armchair in front of it, was a large antique desk. On the desk was a tangle of papers and a telephone. Near its left hand side lay a pair of metal rimmed glasses and a cane. Next to those items sat a three inch diameter cylinder about a foot in length made of stainless steel. A man was just standing up from the leather chair behind the desk.

The Scar grated out, "Going somewhere Mr. Sanderson? Or should I say Sykes?"

Sanderson/Sykes didn't seem surprised. He stood leaning forward, supporting his weight on his hands, "So, it was you who has unleashed my store of Black Fog...I didn't think there was much chance of an accident. Welcome Scar, I'd been expecting you to put in an appearance sooner or later."

The Historical Society director seemed awfully calm to the Purple Scar. Perhaps it was a front while he stalled for time ...or perhaps it was some kind of ruse. The Scar decided to play along, he had questions to ask anyway, "Black Fog? Is that what you call it? Who dreamed it up? You? Paley? Or someone else you have around here?"

Sanderson looked surprised, "Paley? Paley couldn't invent something as complicated as my Fog. It took me years to perfect my formula."

"Where is Paley?' the masked avenger hissed.

Sanderson/Sykes smiled, "Oh, he's around here somewhere." He paused and raised an eyebrow, "You didn't think he was smart enough to be behind my Fog, did you? He's just an ambitious politician, easily distracted by promises of power."

"I did suspect him for a time until I figured out who you really are. It was very clever coming back here disguised as a middle aged historian. You had me fooled...at first. It's too bad that no one looked deeper into your credentials before you were hired. The university listed in your biography never heard of you." The Scar gestured at the glasses and cane with his pistol, "Smart, making yourself look older. If anyone connected all this chaos with the Sykes family, you would be too old to be suspected as the young son returned."

Sykes nodded and reached up one hand to touch his deeply receding hairline, "The glasses were all that was needed. I have mother nature to thank for my premature hair loss, and an auto accident to thank for my limp." He picked up his cane and leaned heavily on it as he took a step from behind the desk.

"Stay where you are! We're going to wait right here for a while," the Scar rasped out.

Sykes nodded again, "So we're expecting visitors, are we? I might have expected it. So...what shall we talk about?"

"Tell me about the Blackness. How does it work?"

Sykes smiled, "Isn't it wonderful? It took years but I finally found a compound that reacts with the moisture in the air to cause my Black Fog. When compressed it becomes a liquid that expands rapidly and reacts with whatever moisture is present. It is especially useful in fog, mist or

"Stay where you are."

even high humidity air such as we're having now. It would be less efficient in dry desert air but is still useful." He shrugged, "I considered selling it to the government and I'm sure they would have paid handsomely for it, but then I realized it would let me return to Akelton and revenge myself on those who killed my father and stole my childhood." The last words were spoken harshly and a cold glitter had come to Syke's eyes.

The Scar was only half listening to his enemy. He could hear shouts, mostly in Spanish, coming from through the open French doors. He was also hoping to hear the sounds of sirens at any minute. To keep Sykes talking he asked, "How does Paley fit in?"

"Paley? Paley is even now waiting upstairs." Syke barked out a mirthless laugh, "All this time he thought he was part of my plan. He's right but not the way he thinks. Things are nearly complete. Now all that is needed is the denouement. There must be villain and a hero."

Understanding the Scar whispered harshly, "So Paley was never meant to win the election. You intend him to take the blame while you walk away cleanly."

Another harsh laugh came from the Master of the Black Fog, "Of course. All his political rhetoric just gave him a good motive. Paley's dead body will be found in the chemical building. He will be blamed and my man will win the election over the disgraced and embarrassed Mayor."

The Scar almost smiled as he saw the subtlety of the plan. Sykes was really backing the forgotten man, the quiet candidate; Ross. He nodded, "So you caused chaos to ruin the Mayor's campaign and get your man elected."

"Oh, it's better than that! My campaign of destruction will pay back the city for allowing my father to be treated the way he was. They took this land; my home for unpaid taxes but my plans will also ruin the Mayor." He laughed out loud, "His ultimate humiliation will be thanking me for saving his life. Yes, the final triumph; I will save the Mayor with Wells to witness our escape. I will be the hero and everyone will praise the new Mayor when he appoints me to fill Paley's council seat." Sykes laughed out loud and shook his free hand as he leaned on his cane, "All this was to happen very soon anyway; your appearance tonight will simply speed up the timetable."

"And the Cubans?"

"I spent some time getting close to the Cuban community in South Florida. I actually was very close to a young lady when I went to school there. Later when I needed soldiers to help me with my plan, I recruited from them. They were perfect. While you and the law were running around chasing local gangs, my Cubans were safely here waiting for the next foray."

The Purple Scar's mind raced. Sykes' plan was complicated but he had carried it out almost perfectly. Still, the Scar had the gun and Griffin should be arriving at the head of a squad of police at any moment. At that instant a huge flash of lightning came from somewhere overhead so bright the Scar blinked for a split second. The crash of thunder followed it by less than a second.

On the heels of the lightning bolt, simultaneous with the wall shaking blast of thunder Sykes threw himself forward his cane swinging. It came down on the Scar's gun arm just above his wrist. He fired as the cane struck. His bullet went beneath Sykes' arm just creasing his ribs. Shattering pain pulsed through his thrice battered arm as his revolver was knocked from his nerveless fingers. Sykes followed this up with a swing at the Scar's head. He saw it coming and ducked under it. As he did he threw a straight left jab that struck Sykes' jaw and sent him staggering back against the desk.

With his right hand still numb, the Scar dove for his revolver lying on the expensive Oriental rug. As he reached it with his left he saw Sykes drop his cane and grab the metal cylinder from the desk. He twisted the valve at one end and threw it at the Scar's head. The masked man ducked and fired with his left hand at the same time. He knew he had missed even as the cylinder now spewing a rapidly growing cloud of Blackness spun over his head. It flew through the doorway into the corridor. The Scar jumped at the door and slammed it closed. As he did he could hear feet on the stairs and a Spanish voice calling out, "Senor! Senor!"

As the door slammed shut with a bang, the Scar spun around with his gun pointed. He was just in time to see a wood panel closing in a corner of the room near the bookcase. Cursing he ran to the wall. The fine wood paneling was featureless at this point. Shoving his gun in a pocket he began running his hands over the paneling feeling for any anomalies.

From the corridor the Scar could hear confused yells. More shouts in Spanish came from the French doors opening to the outside. He gritted his teeth as he continued pressing points on the door. Finally he was rewarded with a click and a narrow section of the paneling pushed inward. Drawing his gun with his left hand the Scar ducked into the dark space. He swung the door closed behind him. His gun in his left hand, he flicked on his pencil flash with his still throbbing right.

He found himself in a two foot wide corridor with unfinished wooden frame and plaster walls on both sides of him. Ahead steps led downward. Seven steps downward the space leveled off. He followed the narrow passage, stooping slightly to duck under a low spot; perhaps a closet or window space in the floor above? The passage continued for another twenty feet before a short flight of steps led upward. The Scar climbed them to a narrow landing where the passage turned sharply to the right. He followed the passage and soon after that it bent back again to the left. Fifteen feet further it bent once again to the right. He had no idea where he was but decided he must be close to the rear of the large building. Finally he faced the rear of a paneled section. A handle protruded from it. Taking a breath he jerked the panel open and light flooded in.

He stood in a large bedroom. Across a canopied bed, Sykes, a leather valise in one hand and a pistol in the other, was just exiting the room. He threw a shot over his shoulder as he ducked through the doorway. His wild shot missed, as did the Scar's left handed return shot. He vaulted across the bed and scrambled in pursuit. Reaching the darkened corridor he flicked off the bedroom light and ducked low into the corridor. Ahead a dimly lit corridor ran straight for nearly the length of the house. The only illumination came from two wide openings to the right. Sykes was just ducking into the first. He noted sourly that the historian seemed to be moving quite well on his supposed bad leg.

As the Scar ran forward revolver up, the lights in the doorways went out. Reaching the first opening he sank down and entered crouched. As he expected he was in the large exhibit room that occupied the center of the second floor, entering opposite where he had first observed the room from. He slid silently toward a dark shadow to use it as cover. As he did, a flash of lightning reflected through the room. With no external windows the flash was subdued but it was enough for the Scar to see movement across the room. To slow his opponent down he threw a shot in that direction; almost immediately his shot was answered.

He paused and stuck his head around the corner of the display he was crouched behind and yelled out in a hoarse voice, "Give it up, Sykes! The police will be here any minute." There was the flash and bang of a pistol shot and the glass display cabinet over his head shattered showering him with glass. His hat and mask protected his face but his position known, the Scar rolled across the floor in the opposite direction in which he had been moving. As he came up against the base of an antique sewing table, Sykes's mocking voice came to him from across the room, "Surrender? You don't accept surrenders. I'll take my chances. My men will be here long before any police, Scar. When the police do get here they'll find your dead body and I'll be an even bigger hero."

As he spoke, Sykes jumped up and ran for a doorway. As he did, he threw two shots wildly in the Scar's direction. The Scar jumped up and ran in pursuit squeezing off one shot that he knew missed in the near darkness. The corridor was lit by a flash of lightning that silhouetted Sykes against a window near the front of the house. The Scar fired twice. His first shot might have clipped Sykes because he cursed and threw himself to the left and crashed through a closed door. His second shot clicked on an empty chamber.

He switched hands with his gun and emptied the shells onto the floor. Feeling was starting to return in his right hand as he dug in his jacket pocket for more cartridges. He moved carefully down the hall as he reloaded. Reaching the corner where he had last seen Sykes he paused. To his right he could hear Spanish-speaking voices floating up from the first floor. Somewhere in that direction was the main staircase. To his left was the darkened doorway Sykes had crashed through. He had taken one careful step toward it when the room beyond was illuminated by another flash of lightning. For a split second he could see that the room was small with multiple windows. Using the crash of following thunder as a distraction, the Scar ducked into the room crouching, his gun up.

Light was better here because the small circular room was lit by three windows set at forty five degrees to each other. He was in one of the circular turrets located at the front of the Sykes mansion. The surprising thing was the small room was empty. The door to the hall had been under his sight the whole time. Sykes must have left another way. The stuffy air in the room indicated that the windows had not been opened recently. There must be another secret passage.

There were only two short internal walls, one to each side of the door. The Purple Scar chose the one to his right and began sweeping his free right hand over the wall. Moments later something moved under his fingers and he pressed firmly. Silently, another narrow panel swung inward.

Light from the windows behind him showed a narrow closet like space. A draft of air came from somewhere above. The Scar stepped forward and felt the rungs of a ladder built to the wall. He shoved his revolver into a pocket and climbed upward. Twelve feet later he reached the end of the chimney-like space. A narrow door yawned open on darkness. He stepped off the ladder onto the third floor and threw himself forward onto the floor as gunfire stabbed from the darkness. Sykes must have been firing blind down the corridor when he heard the Scar on the ladder.

From the floor the Scar fired toward the gun flashes and paused. He laid there for several seconds listening and watching for movement but saw nothing. He did hear distant banging and yells from somewhere in that direction. Crouching, he moved forward cautiously. The corridor was narrower than on the second floor. The only light came from small dormer windows set in the left hand wall. A flash of lightning showed the corridor ahead was empty. He passed several closed doors on his right as he moved forward but ignored them. Finally he reached the approximate spot where Sykes had shot from.

Ahead the Scar could hear yells more clearly now and recognized them as English. Accompanying the yells was the sound of pounding on wood. Another prisoner? Paley, perhaps? He could feel cool fresh air and was just reaching for his pencil flash when a flash of lightning reached down through an open doorway just ahead on his right. A second later the rumbling thunder followed loudly. The lightning flash had illuminated a narrow open doorway to the right. The cool air coming from it indicated an opening to the roof.

The Scar hooked an eye around the corner of the doorway. Dim light from above showed a steep set of stairs leading upwards. Cloudy night sky framed by a rectangular opening could be seen above him. Every instinct he had told him that Sykes was waiting for him above. If he stuck his head onto the roof the phony historian would have a clear shot at him. Instead the Scar flattened himself against the wall next to the doorway, face against the wall and reached around with his foot to the first narrow tread. He pressed down hard with his foot. Nothing happened. He reached out farther and pressed with the toe of his shoe. The old bare wood creaked loudly.

Sykes crouched next to the roof exit leaned in and fired blindly twice down the stairway. The Scar fired around the corner once in reply, making Sykes duck back as he thundered up the stairs firing as he went. He burst out of the horizontal opening and threw himself flat on the roof. Rolling over he saw Sykes running across the flat roof. He fired his last shot into the air and yelled harshly, "Don't move Sykes or you're dead!" Sykes stopped and held his arms straight out to his side. He then turned slowly around as the Scar got to his feet.

Sykes laughed and dropped his empty pistol, its slide locked back, to the roof. The Scar took in their surroundings as he stepped forward. The flat area they stood on was perhaps twenty feet by thirty. A low metal rail ran around the perimeter. It was certainly the widows walk at the top of the Sykes mansion. Sykes spoke resignedly, "I know what happens to people who go up against you, Scar. Go ahead and shoot."

The Scar's reply came harshly, "You thought you could neutralize me with your imported gunmen and clever invention but this is my town, Sykes. Now it's time to pay for what you've done to it." Before Sykes could reply the wail of distant sirens came to the ears of the two adversaries. "That will just about do . . ." The Scar's last words were drowned out by a blinding flash from directly overhead. This time the actual lightning bolt itself was seen arcing downward to strike an ancient oak fifty yards from the mansion. The deafening crash of thunder came almost simultaneously.

Both men threw up hands to shield their eyes but as they did Sykes threw himself toward his foe. The Scar dropped his empty revolver and grabbed at Sykes' hands. As he got a hold on them he fell backwards onto his back. As Sykes left his feet the Scar aided his flight with his knees in his opponent's belly. Sykes flew over the supine Scar and landed with a hard thud on the widows walk and rolled into the railing.

In a flash the Scar was on his feet, hands up. Sykes scrambled up still full of fight and both men closed fists swinging. The Scar led with a left-right combination, pain shooting up his tender right arm as he did. Sykes blocked the first punch but not the second. Fortunately for him the Scar wasn't able to put this full weight behind it. Instead Sykes grunted and backed up a step. The Scar followed up with a series of left jabs to keep his opponent off balance but Sykes ducked most of them and replied with two hard punches to his opponent's stomach.

It was the Scar's turn to grunt and retreat. The two men circled and jabbed looking for an opening. In the background the sirens grew louder. "Do you hear that Sykes? You're out of time," the Scar yelled triumphantly. Goaded Sykes stepped in with a flurry of punches. A couple landed but the Scar blocked most of them and replied with a left to the body and a straight right jab that caused red hot pain to shoot up his arm but landed on Sykes chin and jerked his head back.

Sykes shook his head and snarled, "Damn you Scar! You've ruined everything! It was all perfect! You're stealing my revenge just as those men stole my childhood." As he spoke Sykes stepped in, fists flailing. The Scar retreated. Sykes in his self-righteous fury was out of control. The masked vigilante blocked punches and waited for the right moment. Sykes obligingly stepped in hard with a jab followed by a powerful right hook. The Scar stepped forward brushing inside the jab and dropped to one knee as Sykes' momentum from his right hook swung his body over the Scar's head. He straightened up hard grasping Sykes' thighs with his hands and throwing him over his shoulder. Sykes flew through the air with a scream. The Scar spun just in time to see Sykes fly over the railing.

The Purple Scar paused for a moment in the darkness. Loud police sirens tore the night and reflected headlights came from below at the base of the mansion. As he trudged toward the edge of the widow's walk where Sykes had disappeared, another flash of lightning threw the roof into stark relief. A hand grasped the railing directly in front of him. Nonplussed the Scar leapt forward. Dropping to one knee he grasped the wrist and grated out, "Sykes! Reach up and give me your other hand!" He could see Sykes face in the dim light but couldn't read his expression. The phony historian hesitated for a moment then grabbed at the Scar's free hand. The Scar got a firm hold on this hand and yelled, "Hold on!" He heaved backwards with all his strength, pain lancing through his injured arm.

Another flash came. The Scar didn't hear the closely following clap of thunder as he stared into Sykes' face. Instead of fear, terror or even relief what the saw was a visage filled with hate. Before the Scar could brace himself Sykes pulled his legs up, braced himself against the very steep angled wall of the third floor and pulled downward. With gravity on his enemy's side the Scar couldn't save himself. He catapulted outward into the dark sky.

Releasing Sykes' hands, the masked man twisted in the air and grabbed for the railing as he flashed past it. He missed with his left but got a grip with his right. His outward momentum checked, the Scar's body arced around and slammed into the wall, the impact almost tearing his grip loose. As it was, his arm screamed in pain and a gritted gasp squeezed between his tight lips. Reaching up he got his left hand up to grasp the railing and take some of his weight from his injured arm.

The two men hung there, side by side, forty feet in the air. Unable to use his hands Sykes swung up a foot and kicked the Scar in the side. He grunted and replied with a kick of his own. There were shouts and gunfire from below. The Scar couldn't take his eyes from his opponent but he could hear police whistles and calls in English to surrender. Sykes kicked again. The Scar countered with his knee, blocking this kick. Knowing his right arm would soon give out the Scar began working his hands sideways along the rail, trying to get enough room to boost himself up and over the rail to safety. Sykes crabbed along behind, kicking at his hated adversary as the two edged sideways to the right.

The walls below the widow's walk sloped down at about nearly seventy degrees. Below that was a short roof line about four feet long sloping to a sheer drop. To the Scar's right two steeply angled rooflines met at an inward ninety degree angle at one of the front towers which continued up to a steep, conical rooftop. He had reached the corner of the railing. He stopped and waited. His right arm was throbbing and he felt his grip in that hand weakening. Sykes kicked out at him but barely made contact. His hands slid along the railing and he edged closer.

Lightning flashed. The Scar saw Sykes face twisted in hate as he twisted sideways and brought both legs up. He kicked out and caught Sykes' arm and chest with both feet. Both Sykes' arms were torn from the railing. Simultaneously, the Scar let go of the railing and used the resistance of Sykes body to kick off and push himself sideways away from his opponent. He turned and reached wide with his arms as he landed with a crash in the sharp angle of the roof and the tower wall. As his feet scrabbled for purchase he heard Sykes' scream behind him.

The Scar's feet slid down the slick slate roof but caught in the metal rain gutter. He clung there a moment, took a deep breath and using the converging walls he pushed himself up the steep roof until he was level with the widow's walk. He lunged sideways and caught the railing at waist level. He leveraged himself up and over it to lie on the flat roof. He lay there for a moment getting his breath back as large drops of rain began landing on and around him.

Slowly the Purple Scar pushed himself to his feet and trudged to the edge of the walk. Craning himself forward he could make out several flashlight beams converged on the Master of the Black Fog lying unmoving on the grass near the building. He turned and climbed down the steep stairs to the third floor, stopping only long enough to pick up his fedora and empty revolver from the flat widow's walk. On that floor he ignored the frightened yells of the captive down the hall and worked his way toward the rear of the building. It was easy to find the rear stairwell and his strength returning he quickly dropped down them to the second floor.

He could hear voices in English coming from the front of the house. He hesitated for only a moment as he ducked around a corner looking for the rear stairwell to the first floor. He quickly located it but more voices came to his ears. The Scar could not chance an encounter with the police so he ignored the stairs and instead jerked open the small door set into the wall next to it. Climbing in, he braced his legs against the side walls while he quietly closed the door. Then he simply relaxed his legs and slid down the metal chute.

The chute dropped straight down for fifteen feet then curved and turned horizontal. The Scar was expecting this and he tried to land gracefully as he exited the chute but he was moving fairly fast and he couldn't get his feet under him in time. Instead he dropped off the edge and slid across the basement floor landing hard on his rear. He hopped up immediately thinking to himself that he remembered childhood slides as being gentler.

He immediately started for the corridor leading to the prisoner's cells but stopped cold. Seconds counted if he was to free the prisoners and make his escape but a memory came to his mind as he saw the glow coming from the furnace's grate. Suddenly he laughed out loud and walked up to the hulking mass in the corner of the basement.

Using his gloved hands the Scar reached down and quickly flipped the handle of the grate door and pulled it open. Scorching air and reddish yellow light streamed out. Without hesitating the Scar pulled off his fedora and flicked it into the flames. His tie quickly followed. He shoved his empty revolver into his belt, pulled off its holster and threw that into the furnace. He transferred his trusty master keys and pencil flash to his trouser pockets then tore off his jacket and tossed it into the flames as well. He then reached up with his left hand and ripped off his right shirt sleeve. It tore completely free and quickly followed his other clothing into the fire. Finally he pulled off the horrific purple mask and consigned it to the flames. Lastly went his gloves. He then used the toe of his shoe to push the metal grate closed.

There was one final touch needed for his plan. Murdock lay down on the dusty floor and rolled around a bit. Standing up, he pulled and tore the pocket of his shirt down and left it hanging on his chest. Judging that he looked disreputable enough, Doc nodded and started for the prisoner's hallway. First he swung open the vacant third cell door. Then he swung the first door open and called out, "Anyone in here?" There was a stirring in the darkness and a voice croaked out, "I'm here." Doc felt his way to the Mayor in the dark and helped him to his feet. The prisoner whispered, "Who are you?"

"Miles Murdock. Is that you, your honor?"

"Murdock? We thought you were dead!"

"No, just stuck in a cell for days. C'mon, let's get out of here. Something's going on. I heard gunfire. This is our chance."

In the narrow hallway he felt his way to the last cell, unbolted it and pulled it open, "Anyone here?"

A groan answered Doc's inquiry. Over his shoulder the Mayor gasped, "Who is it?"

Murdock groped his way forward, "Don't know. Give me a hand. We've got to get him out of here." Between them they managed to get Wells on his feet and dragged him out of the cell. Doc led the way back to the furnace room. It wasn't much lighter here than in the cell block but there was enough light for Doc to point out the exterior cellar doors. He drew his revolver out of his waistband and pointed with it, "Looks like that's our only way out. Better hope it's not locked." At the foot of the stairs, Doc left Wells in the Mayor's arms and pushed up and out on the doors. Of course, they swung open easily. With both doors folded back he helped get the semi-conscious Wells up the stairs and into the night air.

It was raining; hard. After the stuffiness of the basement and all the physical exertions he had gone through in the last half hour Doc thought the rain felt like liquid gold. As the trio walked slowly toward the front of the house a police officer came around the side of the house with flashlight and drawn weapon. He caught sight of the three men and hit them with the flashlight beam, "Don't move. Hold it right…My God! It's the Mayor." He lifted his whistle and began blowing short blasts on it. Seconds later uniformed officers were swarming around. As Doc handed the injured Wells off to a couple of officers he tried to keep from smiling. Sykes had been correct; his escape had worked perfectly.

Things were a little confused for a while. Apparently Griffin had brought every peace officer in three counties, or so it seemed. There were certainly plenty of uniforms and guns around. On the heels of the police came ambulances. There were several casualties among Sykes' Cuban gunmen. Doc was very interested to see a couple of beat up looking men being carried on stretchers up from the county road. It seemed there had been some sort of traffic accident just outside the gates of the new Museum. Some oxygen and fresh water soon brought Wells around. Of course he was furious to find himself strapped to a stretcher and unable to run around interviewing people. Before he was transported away in the same ambulance as the Mayor, Doc Murdock stopped to say goodbye. The Mayor had been most gracious, thanking Doc and shaking his hand vigorously. Even Wells had given him a sincere "Thank you."

Now things were settling down. Doc sat on the tail of an ambulance while an attendant eased his bandaged arm into a sling. When he was finished the attendant urged him to see a doctor as soon as he got back to town. Doc tried not to laugh out loud at the irony. He made way for the attendant to look at a wounded Cuban in hand cuffs and ran smack into Griffin. The Captain of Detectives looked tired but pleased. When he saw

Doc his smile faded quickly, "Miles, are you alright? You look terrible."

Doc smiled tiredly, "I've been better. But at least I'm in one piece."

Griffin nodded while eyeing Doc's bruised face and injured arm, "That's more than we can say about some people. We're still scraping Sanderson's body up. I can't believe he was behind all this mess."

Doc glanced around and lowered his voice, "Yes, it's hard to believe that he's the young Sykes boy, but I heard it from his own mouth. He's been planning his elaborate revenge for years. The Blackness, the gunmen, Paley, everything; the whole complicated plan . . ." Doc trailed off and looked thoughtful before continuing, "And he almost pulled it off. It was a near thing, Dan." He shook his head tiredly.

The gruff detective placed a gentle hand on the physician's shoulder, "Thanks to you, Miles. Sanderson had us all so off balance that only the Purple Scar could have figured this out." He smiled, "I guess he should have done his homework and known how the Purple Scar reacts to threats."

Murdock looked at him curiously for a moment then shook his head tiredly, "He said something like that near the end." He brooded for a moment but was interrupted by a voice, "Captain Griffin! Help!" Dan Griffin and Doc turned as Councilman Paley was led away in hand cuffs by two police officers. Neither man said a word as Paley was shoved into the back of a squad car still protesting his innocence. Griffin shook his head, "Paley was in on it too. I can't believe it."

Doc hated to bring up any more bad news but it needed to be said, "Unfortunately he wasn't the only one. Ross was Sykes' man on the Council. He was working quietly to get Ross elected. He intended to pin the whole mess on Paley and then look like a hero by saving the Mayor and Wells. With both Paley and the Mayor discredited, Ross would have been elected easily. Then Sykes would be sitting pretty."

Griffin wiped a tired hand over his face, "Ross, too? Anyone else? Do I have to go home and question my wife as well?"

Doc just stared at something unseen in the distance, "I told you, he was planning this for years. Say Dan, do you think I can get a ride home, I could use some sleep…and Dale will be worrying."

"Hang on a minute and I'll drive you myself. The chief wants a report right away. I'll come back out here later to wrap things up. I told the boys to radio the station that all the captives were safe, including you."

Murdock nodded his thanks. Soon he was sitting in a cruiser next to Griffin driving down to the county road. There, spotlights had been set up and a tow truck was pulling something unseen from the bushes by winch.

Griffin remarked off handedly, "It seems some of Sykes' men drove off the road down there...you wouldn't know anything about that, would you?" There was no answer. As he accelerated down the county road toward town Griffin looked at the man next to him. Doc, his head leaned back against the cushion, was asleep. Griffin smiled and drove on toward Akelton.

CHAPTER NINETEEN

The following Saturday, Doctor Miles Murdock was in his Swank Street apartment struggling with his tie. He had tossed the sling away the day before but his arm was still splinted. His doctor had told him he had only a hairline fracture and would heal quickly but he still had to wear the splint for another fortnight. He had opened both clinics up again this week, for consultations only, but it was still wonderful to get back to work. The only real problems he was having were tying his shoes and ties.

At that moment he heard footsteps on the stairs and Dale breezed into the room. She saw Doc standing in front of the mirror and smiled, "We're going to be late for our brunch reservation if we don't get a move on, mister." Doc gave her a "help me" look and she set down her purse and walked over and gently re-tied his striped tie, "There. That will do." She looked around, "Where's Tommy?"

"He's taking a couple of days off now that he has the use of his arm back." Doc waved his injured arm in frustration.

Dale remarked innocently, "That's too bad. You two looked so good in matching slings. But if Tommy's not here who's going to tie your shoes?"

Doc tried to look superior as he motioned at his feet with his good hand, "Loafers."

"It's amazing how resourceful you are," she marveled.

"Only when I really need to be."

Dale laughed as she picked up her purse and led the way downstairs. The two exited the front door of the clinic onto Swank Street where Dale had parked her car. She got behind the wheel while Doc took the passenger seat. As she pressed the starter Dale remarked, "I'd almost forgotten what it's like to actually leave through the front door."

Doc nodded, "After a while you get used to going in through alleys and windows."

Dale gave him a disapproving look, "Speak for yourself."

The drive downtown was pleasant but slow. The entire downtown area was alive with activity. Stores were open and traffic was heavy. Many pedestrians strolled the streets greeting shop keepers and other passersby. The only police they saw was one lone beat cop walking along swinging his night stick as if he hadn't a care in the world.

"Looks like Akelton is bouncing back quickly," Dale remarked.

Doc agreed, "It's good to see after all this town has been through."

"Things do seem to be getting back to normal. I see where Paley is being indicted for working with Sanderson, uh I mean Sykes."

"Yes, Dan Griffin says they found plenty of evidence at the mansion implicating both he and Councilman Ross, who is also being indicted."

At a stop light Dale looked at her fiancé. "Well, the mayor certainly thinks you're a hero. Are you going to accept the City Council seat that he's offered?"

Murdock looked pained, "Are you serious? After what we've just gone through, the last thing I want is to get involved in politics." Dale laughed heartily as the light changed and they drove on. Doc thoughtfully added, "Although I wouldn't mind working with the Historical Society. We're going to need a new director."

Dale spoke severely, "Just see that they do a better job picking the new one than they did the last. Say, speaking of Sykes; what's going to happen to his formula for the Blackness?"

Doc shrugged, "Dan says the Government has stepped in and confiscated everything concerning the Blackness as a matter of 'National Security,' not that it's likely to do them any good."

When Dale looked surprised Doc continued, "Sykes' papers have been searched thoroughly. There are tons of notes concerning his research but nothing specific to the Blackness. Certainly no formula has been found. Sykes probably kept that in his head." He shrugged again, "Since the main store of chemical was vaporized into the air, the only samples left are small amounts in a couple of the man sized units." He shrugged, "That's not much to work with. It's possible that the formula is lost forever."

"Maybe it's just as well," Dales said soberly. Doc nodded thoughtfully.

As they pulled over and parked, Dale asked, "What's going to happen to the museum?"

Doc smiled at her as he opened his door, "It still belongs to the city and outside of a few bullet holes in the walls it's in great shape. Sykes did create a fine local museum. It will make a nice tourist attraction."

As the two walked up the street to the restaurant, Doc realized it was the same restaurant where he had been waiting for Dale the first night the Blackness had descended on Akelton, "God knows the city certainly deserves something good to come of all this."

Something about his tone struck Dale and she caught his good arm and pulled him around to look in his eyes. Miles looked tired she thought, "Are you alright?"

Doc gave her a weak smile, ""It was a rough week. I guess I am tired."

Dale reached up and touched her fiancé gently on the cheek, "Akelton wouldn't have made it through without you."

Doc nodded and gestured at the busy street, "I guess it was worth it."

Dale pulled him toward the restaurant door, "C'mon. Let's have some champagne and start the healing right now; Doctor's orders."

Miles Murdock knew better than to argue. He let himself be led into the restaurant, "Always do what the doctor says."

THE END

ABOUT OUR CREATORS

AUTHOR

GENE MOYERS —From his lair deep in the forests of the Pacific Northwest Gene, closely watched over by his wife and two always hungry Belgian Sheepdogs, cranks out various scribblings on his old manual typewriter. His somewhat disjointed thoughts have been published in a variety of Airship 27 books including Domino Lady, Phantom Detective, Moon Man, Ravenwood and Purple Scar. He has also been published by Pro Se Press and Moonstone Books.

This book, his first full novel is dedicated to his "Boss," partner and soulmate Felicia. If you liked this book let him know. If you didn't…let him know anyway.

COVER ARTIST

GRAHAM HILL - Sometime Comic-book cover artist for small press publishing companies. Recently completed covers for BLUEWATER COMICS on their Freddie Mercury (Queen front man), David Bowie and other graphic novels. (Brain May from the band Queen apparently liked the Freddie one…not sure what the "Thin White Duke" thought of his …) Covers for magazines such as SIMIAN SCROLLS, APE CHRONICLES, BLOKES TERRIBLE TOMB OF TERROR. Earned a first class BA (Hons) degree in fine art many years ago when I had more hair. Can be found on Face Book where I sometimes go under the Pseudonym of "Cover Monkey" https://www.facebook.com/CoverMonkeyGrahamHill.

INTERIOR ILLUSTRATIONS

CHRIS KOHLER - Comics, and the creation of such, have been an obsession for most of my life. Many years had been spent trying to be the next John Byrne (or at least, the next Sal Buscema…) while floundering for some sort of direction and style to go along with the passion. Several more years were spent doing everything *but* drawing.

Finally at age 30, there was a synergy between the discipline required in order to draw and the joy felt due to drawing. Since then, a couple hundred pages of comics or so have been born between short stories for small press groups such as Hidden Agenda Press and Approbation Comics, and commissioned pieces done via eBay and deviantArt.

From 2009-2013, I worked with writer Daniel VanderMolen on my largest work to date (over 80 pages), a zombie strip called *Portland Underground* (www.pdxunderground.net). Another couple of years were spent creating 32 pages of EC-style shorts with writer Larry King (no relation!), to be published at a later date under the title of '*Tales of Woe*'.

In addition to small press & web comic work, I've been doing interior illustrations for New Pulp publications such as Van Plexico's entire *Sentinels* novel series (8 books so far), and a couple of one-off collections such as *Blackthorn* and *The Many Worlds of Ulysses King*.

HORROR HAS A NEW FACE

From the pages of the classic pulps comes the most frightening avenger of them all, the Purple Scar!

The handsome, debonair Dr. Miles Murdoch was a world famous plastic surgeon. His life was the stuff of dreams until it all turned into a heart-wrenching nightmare. Murdoch's brother, a dedicated police officer, is brutally gunned down while on patrol. Before dumping his body into the river, his murderers pour acid over his face as a final act of contempt. When the body washes ashore days later, Officer Murdoch's face is beyond recognition, a scarred, purple visage unlike any horror ever imagined.

It is the sight of this death grimace that transforms Miles Murdoch into an avenging angel. Vowing to bring justice to those responsible, the skilled surgeon molds a pliable rubber mask from that repulsive, mutilated face; a mask he dons to become the Purple Scar, the scourge of crooks and villains everywhere. He has become the physical embodiment of their worst fears brought to fiendish life.

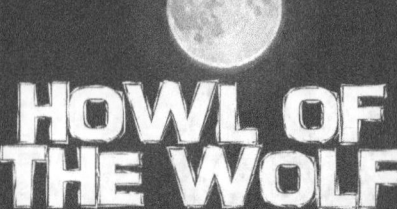

www.ingramcontent.com/pod-product-compliance
Lightning Source LLC
Chambersburg PA
CBHW070816250626
47170CB00006B/2127